Animal

Animal

L. J. Bomba

L. J. Bomba

Typesetting services by BOOKOW.COM

To the many teachers, professors, friends, and family who have cheered me on along the way

Thank you

Preface

This book came about through many years, many sleepless nights in college, and through many hardships. It was a wild ride built on numerous experiences- both good and bad- that have made up much of my life

Those experiences built this story, a story I now present to you.

Acknowledgments

Edited By: Alice Martinez

Contents

Experiment 1 | Father

When I was born none of the doctors were surprised by pointed ears, the warm crimson eyes, or the small tuft of fur sticking out of my backside. No, all of this went according to plan. Who's plan? My father who was experimenting with gene splicing to improve the human race. I was to be a final attempt to obtain the outcome he so desperately craved.

By all accounts I was a success, but my early life would prove otherwise. When I was finally old enough and had learned enough to coherently provide answers for testing, they began to examine me closely. It was when I turned five that it dawned on me that the test was all that mattered to father.

First, they would test my senses to see how "enhanced" I had become. My eyes were miserable. I couldn't see color to its fullest, it was faint and dull and I hated it. The only exception seemed to be the brightest reds which seemed to glow in my boring world.

But when they tested my ears, I could hear everything. There were frequencies they insisted that humans simply couldn't hear, but I could hear it, couldn't I? That's when I realized I wasn't human. I wasn't like everyone else in those small claustrophobic rooms. I was alone.

Sometime thereafter, my father insisted they examine my physical prowess. This was also around the time that my claws grew in instead of the nails I thought were mine. I looked even further from what I sought to be. After a test of endurance, climbing, and strength it was determined that I was hardly any better than the average child of my age. That made me so delighted to hear from them; something about me was normal.

Alas my father was anything but pleased, and he took his frustrations out on me. When he first hit me, I was so taken aback that it didn't even register in my mind. There was blood across my face even before it dawned on me. I knew my father hated me, but I just couldn't grasp what it was that I had done to him. Around that time, I moved in to where my father was living. It was so different from what I had grown used to; the entrance area of his house was bigger than the only room I had known.

"Father, this is your home?"

"It's your home too starting today so you better get used to it."

It was my home? I felt an urge deep in my heart to embrace my father, but I knew he hated when I touched him. I followed him as he turned to go up a staircase towards what I would learn was the attic.

"This is your room from now on."

My heart dropped faintly as I entered the room. It was barely bigger than the cell I had known all my life and it was miserably plain. No colors reflected off the walls, the bed had no blanket and no patterns on the sheets, and it was where I would be living from then on.

"You'll be starting school in a few weeks. You better not make a fool of me."

"School, father? What about our tests?"

"They will be happening monthly from now on."

With that he turned and exited the room, closing the door with a click as he did so. Just like that, I was alone with nothing to do. Test once a month? What was I supposed to do until then? Before the day was through, I realized just how dreadful the wait for school would become in that little dull room. As time slowly dragged on, I found myself dragging my claws along the walls and floors scraping at them slowly.

It occurred to me that even without supplies I had something to do and began to draw all across my room with carvings. I had already drawn several pictures of myself and father by the time dinner came around, but it was different. In them I wasn't what I was. I was human. A knock arrived at my door and I quickly stood and brushed my claws on my pants.

"Dinner."

There stood father with a hand outstretched like I had never seen it. I slowly walked over to it and lifted my hand to grasp it only for him to grab me first and drag me along down the hall. When he stopped tugging at my arm, I saw that we had entered a fanciful looking room with a large table at its center. Compared to the thin metal dish that I was fed from before, it was simply magical.

"T- this is where we are eating...?"

Smack!

"Don't stutter. Sit."

Hurriedly, I pulled myself off the floor and sat in one of the many chairs that lined the table. Manners had been something that I was taught very early on in case I had to be paraded around to potential buyers of whatever I was. I waited quietly for food to be sat in front of me, but it didn't seem to be coming. Just as I began to think I wouldn't be eating that evening a plate was set in front of me by a woman I had never seen.

"There you are ma'am."

"Ma'am?"

Slap!

"Sorry. Thank you very much."

I sat anxiously waiting for my father to take the first bite before I dared to touch mine. Then he started to eat as I slowly lifted my fork and moved it towards the dish. Eating at tables had always felt tedious to me; eating with one's hands was easier. Yet, without much thought about the flavor of the food, I ate. When I was finished my father dragged me right back to my room.

That is how my days went for the remaining week before school would inevitably begin. On that day, I was quickly made to dress up in a formal uniform and set up with a lunch box before being driven down the way to the school by the woman I still hadn't been introduced to. All I had been able to put together is that she was hired help of some sort.

As the car pulled into the roundabout of the school, I started to feel nervous. There were so many people all around. At most I had spent time around maybe four people; what was father thinking?

"Are you alright?"

I simply nodded in response to her question and then flinched as I realized my mistake.

"Hey, calm down, I'm not going to hurt you. Worried?"

"Yeah."

"I was worried on my first day of school too."

She looked down at my tail that sat in my lap as she said so.

"You know when I attended school, I had a secret weapon."

"A- a weapon...?"

The only weapons I knew of were the violent kinds.

"Yup-" she pointed to a flower pin on her lapel "This here got me through everything."

"Really?"

She smiled warmly at me as she undid the pin from her jacket and pinned it to my dress.

"And now it can help you too."

I set a hand on the ruby red flower now resting on my uniform.

"I- I shouldn't take this, what if something happens?"

"It's not a big deal, now run along so you aren't late on your first day."

Quickly, I got out of the car and pulled my bag over my shoulder as I turned to face the school. Oh! I turned to the car to say thank you to the lady for the charm only to see she had already gone. Looking back to the school, I took a deep breath and began walking towards the entrance with my tail hanging low behind me.

Experiment 2 | 1st Day of School

As I entered the building for my first day, I quickly realized I wasn't sure where I was supposed to go. I found myself standing there just ahead of the entrance not knowing what to do. As people passed by me, I began to notice many of them were staring. It occurred to me that they hadn't seen anything like me before. Then, while I was stuck in my own head, I felt a tap on my shoulder.

"Hello little girl, are you lost?"

There was a lady standing over me with a smile. I nodded hesitantly.

"Do you know who your teacher is?"

I shook my head steadily.

"Do you have your folder in your bag?"

Hurriedly, I removed my bag from my back and opened it quickly pulling a plain brown folder out of it. I held it up to her without saying anything.

"May I look in it?"

I nodded and she took it from my hand and opened it.

"Let's see here, ah here we are, you are in Ms. Margaret's classroom. Walk with me and I can take you there."

I walked behind her quietly while clutching my bag, other children who were walking through the halls continued to watch me as I continued. Two hallways down, we turned to the left and entered one of the rooms where several of my peers already sat ready to learn. As I continued to follow the woman to the front of the class, I saw that another woman who I assumed was Ms. Margaret ahead of us.

"Hello. Who's this with you, Lyle?"

"This is going to be one of your students this year."

I saw Ms. Margaret peek around to catch a glance at me as I hid behind Ms. Lyle.

"Oh! You must be Nym?"

I frantically shook my head.

"No?"

She glanced over the stack of papers on her clipboard.

"It says here that you're Nym, unless there is another student with a tail I am expecting?"

I turned away from her and hid my face while grabbing at my tail.

"Hey, I didn't mean to upset you. I just meant that I was told you would be joining us and that your name was Nym."

"I- I don't have a name, I'm just called 'Subject 17' usually..."

I crept even further behind Lyle as I spoke, worried that I would be in trouble for trying to correct a teacher. From what I could barely see, they exchanged a nervous glance between each other.

"Well here if you would like you can go by Nym? It's what is written here after all."

I nodded shakily, still waiting for someone to yell or hurt me.

"Ok Nym," she got down to my level and stuck out her hand. "Should we introduce you to the class?"

I stole a glance at the children now lining the desk, still looking at me. Then, with a lump in my throat, I nodded and let her lead me to the front of the room.

"Class this is Nym. She'll be joining us for the rest of the school year. She may look a bit different from all of you, but I expect each of you to treat her well."

Someone in class raised their hand.

"What is she?"

I could tell by the cadence in their voice that they had no foul intentions and were likely just curious, but it still stung. I went to answer all the same.

"I'm a human. But I have also been spliced."

From the reaction of the room, I could tell that no one understood what I meant.

"Sorry, it means that I have parts in me that aren't human."

Still, everyone seemed mostly puzzled but the teacher continued anyway.

"Ok Nym, you may find your seat now."

I nodded and walked to the back of the class, sitting on the ground. From how everyone was looking at me, I could tell that this was the incorrect response. I had never been in a classroom before but I imagined the environment would be like the lab and test chamber I was raised in.

"Nym you can sit in one of the empty chairs if you want."

I blinked and looked to her, then to the rest of the room. With a bit of hesitation, I stood and glanced at the empty chairs. It was difficult to choose which of them I should sit in.

"Psst- Hey, wolf girl, come over here."

My eyes moved to the girl who had called me over. She had an empty chair next to her so I decided to slowly walk over and sit down. Just like that, the class began to go over things. It wouldn't be long before I realized that I was actually ahead of the curriculum in the school (at least in most cases). As it was, the first day was very boring until lunch time came around.

"So, Nym was it?"

"I guess."

"My name is Chloe. It's nice to meet you."

"Um, it's nice to meet you too?"

"You sound like you aren't sure it is?"

"Sorry, aside from people testing me and some brief lessons I don't really socialize with people much."

"You know you say a lot of smart things!"

"I do?"

She nodded knowingly.

"Yeah! Like 'splicing' and 'socialize'. Very smart things."

"Is it? I just thought that was normal."

"Maybe when kids grow up, I guess."

We continued to talk through lunch and I felt genuinely happy to have made a friend for the first time in my life. But after what felt like a brief lunch, we went back to learning which was just boring again. I hadn't known what to expect from school, but all and all I didn't hate being there. It was preferable to being at home in my room anyway. While I was thinking, the day had flown by and the bell rang. It was piercingly loud and I covered my ears tightly. Then I felt a tap from beside me.

"Hey Nym, are you ok?"

I turned to Chloe and nodded.

"Sorry, loud noises bother me because my ears are sensitive."

"Wow really? That's super cool! So, you have like crazy good hearing then?"

"I guess better than a lot of people."

In my thoughts, it was hard to imagine how others experienced the world.

"Can I ask something that's maybe a bit personal?"

I turned towards her and nodded faintly.

"Yeah, we're friends after all."

"So um, how does it feel to have a tail?"

She gestured towards my tail behind me, causing me to notice it wagging side to side rapidly. Quickly I grabbed hold of it to try to get it to stop moving. My cheeks were probably glowing.

"I don't really know how to describe it. I guess it's not that different from fingers or toes? It just kind of moves sometimes though."

"I guess I would have thought you'd know more about your tail?"

"I just know that it moves differently based on my feelings."

"Like a puppy!"

We both looked at each other before starting to laugh. Finally, we both began to leave the classroom and head our separate ways. By the end of my first day, I thought school would be the best thing in my life.

Experiment 3 | Mary

When I arrived at the car to be taken home, I found the woman from that morning waiting for me. It was then I thought that I should maybe ask her what her name was like Chloe did to me.

"Excuse me, ma'am, what is your name?"

She seemed a bit surprised as though I asked something outrageous.

"You needn't call me ma'am ever, but if you'd like you can call me Maribelle or Mary if you prefer."

"Mary? It's a pleasure to meet you. I'm Nym."

Like the teacher had done earlier, I stuck out my hand to her and smiled widely. She let out a bit of a chuckle through a stunned look and took my hand.

"The pleasure is all mine Nym. So, I see you found out about your name?"

"Yup, though I have to wonder why I never knew it before now?"

At that she gave a weak smile then turned her attention to the road as we went back towards my father's manor. I hadn't noticed it that morning, but our house was not very close to the school at all. It was maybe thirty or forty minutes before we came to the main gate that led up the drive. When we finally arrived at the front door, I entered ready to tell my father of the day's events. But it became apparent all too quickly that talk wouldn't be happening at all.

Just as it had been in the weeks leading up to school, I was led straight back to my room with the door locked behind me. For the life of me I couldn't figure out why my father was so intent on keeping me there. Before I could think about it much longer, I remembered my homework for the day and pulled my writing notebook out of my bag. Writing was so exciting to be trying; I always knew of it because I've seen the little scribbles all over, but no one bothered to teach me.

So, I turned to the first page which had lines for practicing the letter 'A'. I grabbed a pencil from my bag and began to copy the letters. Alas, it seemed like no matter how I handled it I couldn't make a good-looking letter. It would be frustrating if I couldn't pick it up quickly, other students had even already begun writing. Just like that, one page became two and two became ten until I eventually completed the entire alphabet. They all looked so ugly and jagged compared to what they were meant to look like, but I figured the teacher wouldn't mind it.

Knock knock

"Nym, it's time for your dinner."

I stood from the floor and walked over to the door as it opened revealing Miss Mary.

"Hello Miss Mary!"

"Good evening Nym. So, we're going with 'Miss' now huh?"

I nodded happily as we walked down stairs towards the dining room. When we entered, I saw that my father still wasn't around. It suddenly felt as though I wouldn't be telling anyone about my day. Perhaps seeing how disheartened I was, Mary pulled a chair up next to me.

"What's the matter Nym?"

"Oh no, I just... I never thought I would want to tell anyone about my day... especially not my father, but now..."

"Now you actually have something you want to tell?"

I nodded solemnly.

"Well, I know it's not quite the same, but you can tell me how things went if you want?"

With her offer, I began hearing my tail tap on my chair and held it down. Then I told her all that happened on my first day of school. It was so nice to tell someone all that happened to me and how everyone was so kind. As I finished reciting my tale, the door behind us flung open and she quickly sprung to her feet.

"What's this?"

"Father. I was just-"

"Did I address you?"

"No, sir."

"Now then, what were you two doing?"

"Sir, I was just sitting with your daughter because she was feeling a bit lonely."

My father snorted a bit.

"This thing is *not* my daughter; it's only living here so I could keep an eye on it."

My heart ached in my chest. I knew my father didn't care for me, but I at least thought he knew me as his daughter.

"Sir! She's a little girl!"

"Are you raising your voice to me?"

Mary bit her lip.

"No sir, sorry sir."

"I thought so. As for that, it's hardly a little girl."

Tears finally fell from my eyes and I quickly stood from the table, hurriedly walking back to my room. I knew tears would mean a punishment if he saw them.

"Where are you off to?"

"M- my room, sir. M- may I be-"

Whack!

His hand came down on the side of my cheek and I collapsed to the ground.

"What have I said about- are those tears I see?"

"N- no! No sir they aren't!"

Whack!

Another hand came across my face.

"Please don't do this!"

But it was too late. Father clamped a collar onto my throat and dragged me along by a chain into another room with locks fitted to the wall and locked me to it. I had experienced this many times when I was younger, but it had been over a year and it never got easier to stand.

"Now you'll stay here a bit until you learn to behave like a young lady instead of a beast."

Knowing there was nothing I could do at this point and fully aware that any more resistance would just lead to more pain, I fell back on the wall. My eyes were still watery but I wiped at them repeatedly, accidentally cutting my face as I did so. It didn't matter. As long as this punishment was it, I could get through it.

So, there I sat as time passed. First an hour then two, it felt late and I was finally dowsing off when I heard the door to the chamber open slowly. I tried to force myself up so that I wouldn't get scolded more than I already had only to see Mary standing there. As she saw me, her hands flew up to her mouth.

"God Nym are you alright?"

"Y- yeah I'm ok, just a bit tired."

"Sit down and let me look at your cheeks. Can't have you going to school like that can we?"

I let a grin slip onto my face as I thought about seeing Chloe in the morning. Shortly thereafter, Mary returned with some medical supplies. She applied a cleaning solution to my bruises and the cut I had left myself under my eye. Then she put a patch over my bruised cheek and a small bandage over my cut.

"There, that should do it, now you'll feel much better by morning. I also brought you this."

There in her arms sat a small stuffed wolf that I had when I was very young.

"Wait, you can't do all this. He'll know you did it and you'll get in trouble."

Without a word she set my wolf in my arms and turned to leave me. A new fear gripped me that come morning, Miss Mary wouldn't be working here any longer. With that pitiful thought in my mind, I finally collapsed from exhaustion.

Experiment 4 | Art Class

I slowly drifted out of sleep as the morning light crept into my window. What? Where was I? My bed? I sat up and looked around me but didn't find anything out of the ordinary. That was until I realized that my old wolf was clutched beneath my arm. So then last night did happen. But then who carried me here? Surely it wasn't my father, and I thought Miss Mary left last night. But before I could think about it any longer, I heard a tap at my door.

"Nym? You better get up and get ready or you'll be late to school."

"Mary?"

Though no one answered, the light steps leaving my door confirmed to me it was her. She was right though, I needed to get ready if I wanted to make it to school. And oh did I want to make it. So quick as I could, I pulled off my clothes from the night before and dressed myself in my uniform. Then I went to pack up my bag only to find it had already been packed. A grin crossed my face as I pulled the bag onto my shoulder and hurried out the door.

Breakfast with my father was the quietest it had been in some time but I didn't mind. At least if he was quiet, it would mean that he wouldn't be yelling. Just as quick as I had gotten ready, I also finished eating and started to make my way to the front door. But as I passed my father's chair, his hand sprung out to me. His hand was as tight as I expected when it wrapped around my arm, but even the thought of the night before was enough to make me panic.

"You're forgetting something."

He gestured towards the side of the table I had been eating on and saw my lunchbox had been sitting there.

"Sorry sir, I'll get it right away."

With just a nod he released me to hurry over to it and stuff it in my bag. Then as I had tried once before, I walked quickly to the door. As I stepped into the car, I let out a sigh of relief. I was almost certain I was in for another beating so quickly.

"Good morning, Nym."

Mary looked over to me smiling happily.

"Good morning, Miss Mary."

I suddenly remembered what she had done last night.

"Miss Mary, are you alright? Did father... Did he do anything to you?"

"Don't you worry about that Nym. Your father was actually very pleased that I cleaned you up and took you to bed. After all, it would reflect poorly on him if you didn't show up or looked terrible in class, no?"

I understood now. If she had a good reason in his eyes, it didn't matter what she did.

"Speaking of how you look, let me get a good look at you."

She took my head and turned it from one side to another and then removed one bandage after another.

"Ok, besides the cut everything looks about alright."

I pulled down the car's mirror and looked at myself in it. Sure enough, the small nick from my claws sat just beneath my right eye and still looked moderately fresh.

"It's alright there Nym, you can just tell the kids you fell while playing if you'd like?"

I shook my head.

"Not like he did this to me anyways, that one's my fault."

"Right."

With that we pulled up to the school and I was dropped off much like the day before. Except unlike last time,

I knew exactly where I was heading and showed up in class without much trouble. There sat Chloe just as she was yesterday.

"Hey Nym!"

She waved for a moment before cocking her head slightly.

"What happened to your cheek?"

I brushed my hand through my hair and felt sickly.

"I, um, accidentally cut it with my claws."

Her eyes lit up as I said it but she soon realized I was quite ashamed of it and they subsided.

"Your claws must be really sharp huh? Must be rough to deal with them."

I bit my lip while holding in tears.

"Y- yeah, it can be really hard sometimes."

I rubbed at my eyes.

"Oh Nym, hey, it's ok!"

She wrapped her arm around me and let me lay my head on her shoulder as she brushed her hand through my hair.

"You know what will cheer you up a bit?"

I turned my gaze towards her.

"We have art class today!"

"Art class?"

Just as she said, following lunch we weren't returned to our classroom like we had been the day before but were instead led to a different room. We sat as the teacher handed out paper and plates with varying shades of gray stuff across it; I only realized it was colors from the warm red that sat amongst them. Then she gave each of us a brush and told us to paint something.

Confused, I looked down at my paper then to the people around me who already started. Chloe seemed to be in her element as she brushed several of the paints across her paper. I couldn't quite make out what she was painting because it all seemed to blend together. Finally, I turned towards my paper and started smudging some of the red on it. After about an hour the teacher clapped her hands and had us switch paintings with someone to discuss the art. Chloe happily turned to me and held out her paper. I was more hesitant but, in the end, I handed her mine too.

As I looked at her picture, I realized I wouldn't be able to give much feedback. From what I could tell there were two people in the picture but I could hardly make them or their surroundings out.

"Wow you really like red, don't you?"

I tried to avoid looking at Chloe.

"It's not a bad thing, if red is your favorite color, then that's ok silly."

"I- I um- I can't really see much of anything else..."

She looked at me with her mouth slightly ajar then back to my picture which was covered and varying shades of red to make up my room.

"You mean- then you don't know what I drew do you?"

"I know it's two people maybe?"

"Wow, that's crazy. I'm so sorry Nym. I thought art would cheer you up, I didn't know."

I shrugged lightly.

"It doesn't really matter; it's just how I was born. Nothing can be done about it."

"Nonsense! Next time I'll do mine completely in red so you can look at it!"

She grinned so widely at me that I couldn't help but smile back.

Experiment 5 | Accidents Happen

Following my ride back from school, I was again locked into my room. This time I didn't feel so bad about it though. Home life was better if I was away from my father anyway. When dinner time arrived, Mary was there to show me to the table, and just like the day before it was just the two of us. This time I made a point to eat quickly so I wouldn't have to bump into my father. Luckily, he didn't come home until much later in the evening so I was back in my room before I ever saw him.

As I laid in bed working quietly on what homework I had, I heard a firm knock at my door. Distinctly not Mary. My heart began to pound as the door slowly opened revealing my father behind it. I quickly jumped off my bed and stood up straight.

"Your teacher called me."

"Please sir I didn't do anything wro-"

He raised one of his hands which told me to be silent.

"She merely informed me that I should have disclosed your color blindness to the school. She also recommended getting you some things to help with the problem."

I bit my tongue waiting for things to escalate like they usually did. But instead, he just coughed a bit and set a small crimson bag at the edge of my room before leaving. I slowly began approaching the bag, fearful that there was something more to this than what he said. Nervously, I pulled on the zipper revealing- art supplies? I poured the contents of the bag onto the floor in front of me in confusion. Maroon, crimson, cherry? It was all different shades of red? Crayons, paints, colored pencils, all of it red.

I stumbled back to my bed and sat for a moment lightly squeezing my tail to relax. Surely there is something else? Why didn't he just have Mary bring them if it was just this? I shook off any thoughts that began to fester. This couldn't have been all it was, he would torture me by doing nothing at all. Breathing a sigh of relief, I walked over to pick up everything and returned it all to the bag before setting it next to my backpack. It was nice to finally have something more than the mucky bag I had up to now, but it wasn't big enough in itself to be a school bag. I thought one day I would be able to choose a bag all on my own. With that dream lingering in my mind, I got myself ready for bed.

I had started to get used to waking up and getting dressed for school in the mornings. It was a routine I looked forward to everyday because it would mean leaving my room for a while. As I was finishing my preparations, the expected knock finally arrived and Mary opened the door.

"Well, aren't you a young lady today, didn't even have to wake you."

I knew she was only teasing me, but I felt delighted to have been acknowledged by her. Much like our prior days we quickly went for breakfast and then I grabbed my lunch and we were out the door. In the car my excitement must have been noticeable because Mary mentioned it twice. Apparently, it wasn't normal for a kid to be excited for school though I couldn't fathom why. Then we arrived and I waved her off before heading to my class enthusiastically.

"Nym!"

"Chloe!"

Upon spotting each other we ran into a hug and burst into a fit of giggles.

"Oh, how I've missed you."

"Nym, we see each other every day!"

I nodded and tried to keep up my smile.

"I know we do."

"What's wrong?"

"I just… Can I tell you a secret? Promise not to tell?"

Suddenly she seemed very serious and nodded.

"My father doesn't really like me, so home is really bad sometimes."

"Oh… I'm sorry Nym."

I shook my head.

"It's fine, I'm just glad I finally get to be free, if only a bit."

"What does that mean?"

But before I could answer, the teacher began our lesson for the day. Writing was proving difficult for me over the class period. Everyone else seemed to write out sentences of some sort with maybe a little difficulty but for me it was painful. Every line I wrote made my hand ache and risked me cutting the paper with my claws.

"You're holding your pencil wrong."

I looked over to Chloe who held out their hand as an example.

"I'm fine. I got it."

It may have been petty but I didn't like being corrected even if I knew I was doing something wrong. After all, corrections usually came with punishments.

"Here just let me help."

Chloe grabbed at my hand trying to adjust my grip on the pencil.

"I said I can do it!"

I jerked my hand away from Chloe and went back to my work. Then I noticed it; red. I dropped my pencil as Chloe burst into tears next to me. Her hand had been caught on my claws as I ripped it away from me. I hadn't even noticed it. Everyone turned to look at the scene unfolding before them as I tried to calm Chloe down. Our teacher, who had yet to realize the situation, rushed to the cabinet for a first aid kit.

"Chloe! I'm so sorry- please forgive me!"

But it was no use. Her eyes told me that she was afraid of me and wanted to get away, but was paralyzed. Suddenly I was being lifted from my chair by a teacher from down the hall and was dragged away from my friend. From there, they took me to the nurse. They hadn't put together that I wasn't bleeding and thought I too was injured. When it was discovered that not a drop of blood on my hands was my own, I was dragged to the principal's office where I sat awaiting a punishment I knew was coming.

"Nym Witherspoon"

I was waved into the office by the principal.

"Hello, Nym."

The shock from having hurt my friend was still setting in.

"Do you know what you've done, Nym?"

My eyes remained looking down. Thoughts raced through my mind of what was occurring.

"Nym, if you want to have any hope of remaining at this school, I need some answers."

"I- I don't want to stay here sir."

He took in a breath and leaned back in his chair.

"Is that why you lashed out at Chloe?"

"No! I- I didn't want to- I didn't mean-"

My face fell into my hands and I began to sob violently.

"Nym, you need to talk with me."

"I- it was an accident- I swear it was-"

I was having trouble breathing as the conversation continued. Apparently, Chloe's parents had been called and she was being taken home. Next, they would have to call my father and let him know what happened. I would be suspended for a few days while they figured out what would happen with me next. My happiness that I thought I was building towards was torn away from me with my own hands. My blood stained, beastly hands.

Experiment 6 | Suspension

My ride home with Mary was quiet and solemn. Even Mary knew that after what had happened, there was likely little she could do for me. My whole body quivered as we drove up to the house, but in the end, I knew I deserved whatever was coming my way. Yet the steps echoed as we walked to the door and when we reached it, I couldn't bring myself to open it. I had been sobbing on and off since the incident and found myself sobbing again on the steps. Mary's hand rubbed on my back.

"Nym. It wasn't your fault."

"Yes, it is! It's just like father says! I'm no better than an animal!"

My hands shook just thinking of the pain I had caused.

"Nym, it was an accident."

"It doesn't change anything though... w- if I go back to school Chloe won't be there. All of the kids in my class will be afraid of me. My chance to just be normal... it's gone."

Mary wrapped her arms around me and squeezed me softly.

"Whatever happens, it will be ok."

Mary pushed the door open and walked me inside. As expected, my father sat by the entrance with a disapproving look on his face. If my tail could go any lower, it did in that moment. I couldn't bring myself to look directly at my father.

"So, this is what I get for listening to some of my peers?"

I trembled as the words slowly flowed out of my father's mouth.

"Well? Answer me!"

My hands were now clenched tightly, drawing blood from my palms.

"I'm sorry..."

"What was that?"

"I said I'm sorry! You were right! I don't deserve t-"
Smack!

I knew what would come for me if I raised my voice, but unlike usual I wanted the pain, I deserved it.

"How my wife could have given birth to such a useless creature I can't understand."

"It's not like I wanted to be born this way!"

Smack!

My feet gave way beneath me and I stumbled to the floor.

"You think it matters what you want? I wanted you to be a better human. Instead, I get the worst of the things I put into you!"

"Why did you let me live past that? If you knew w-"

His hand wrapped around my jaw.

"You think I want to kill my wife's child?!"

He inhaled deeply before throwing me to the ground again.

"So why won't you be my father?!"

Without looking at me, he turned away and began walking to his study.

"Take that thing back to its room."

Mary came over to me and scooped me off the floor. I had bruises all over and my hands were still bleeding. Up the stairs we went towards my room where she set me on my bed and began work on fixing me up.

"You really shouldn't antagonize him."

"I just really wanted to say some of that... and I deserved to be hit this time anyways."

She looked at me and frowned a bit as she stroked my hair.

"Why- why couldn't I have had a father who loves me ...?"

"Oh Nym, you don't understand now, but that man has had a difficult, bitter life. Nothing ever seems to go right for him. Then this most recent project was going so well when you were born. He even used to be so happy to see you..."

My eyes were fixated on her as I was drawn into her story.

"Then what happened?"

"The test happened. Unfortunately, nothing with them went right. Everything he thought would be there wasn't and he didn't know who to blame."

I realized I wouldn't like this story after all as she continued.

"After that they canceled the closed program test. They wanted to see how you would do in the wild so to speak. But your father's already lost faith and sadly I think he blames you for his own failures."

"Oh..."

She lifted her hand to finish bandaging my face while her words sunk in. It was so much to take in. Now I had a reason for why my father didn't want me. He feels no different about me than how I feel about myself. I was broken, and I didn't need to be here anymore.

"There, all cleaned up and ready to go."

Perhaps realizing I had stopped paying attention, Mary grabbed my arm.

"Don't dwell on it too much. I know it doesn't seem like it, but I think somewhere in that foul old man there is love for you."

She turned to leave my room and clicked the lights off as she did so. Taking some breaths, I leaned back into bed. It was probably just something she was saying, but somewhere in me, I hoped she was telling the truth.

My suspension started the next morning and it was as grueling as the weeks leading up to class. No one visited me for most of the day aside from meals and I never saw my father even once. Thinking about a time after my suspension didn't help either since all I could picture is Chloe's terrified look as I cut her. What was left for me? This room? My monthly test? A father who didn't love me?

I let out a sigh as I dug through my bag for something to take my mind off my miserable life. There I found it, the picture that Chloe had drawn for me just a few days prior. I couldn't see it in any way that mattered, but just knowing someone had worked on it for me meant a lot. Now the thoughts felt soured though. I crumpled the paper and threw it aside as I pulled the art supplies from my bag. Then I looked at my carvings from the days prior and got to work.

By the end of the second day of suspension, my entire ceiling was covered in my archaic style art. It likely would have been eerie to anyone else, but to me it was like breathing life into my once cold, lifeless room. When Mary came knocking to check on me for lunch, I invited her in to see my art.

"You did all of this?"

I nodded a bit as I sat on my bed watching her investigate every picture I had made.

"It's wonderful, all of it."

"Thank you, I was just bored is all."

Deep down I knew they were largely rubbish, but I was happy she said she liked them regardless.

"Oh yes, I come with some good news."

I tilted my head slightly as my tail slowly began to wag.

"After some convincing by some anonymous parties you will be allowed back at school tomorrow; baring some unfortunate clauses."

My tail was in full swing now; though I wasn't sure what clauses meant?

Experiment 7 | Back to School

When I awoke the following morning, I felt anxious about heading back to school. It wasn't like my mornings before school on any other day. Now people had an expectation of me and it wasn't a good one. Mary didn't seem much better as we drove to my school, in fact she looked more anxious than I was.

"Ok Nym. Whatever happens today, I want you to promise me you'll keep your head up."

"Keep my head up?"

"Yes. Don't let anyone get you down, what happened before wasn't your fault."

It sure felt like my fault. But I still found it in me to give her a nod as I stepped out of the car and moved slowly to the doors. Everyone around moved several feet away from me as I shakingly stepped into the building. With a deep breath, I continued on to my classroom. I remained in front of the door for a moment, afraid of what I might find there. Just as I raised my hand to enter, A hand tremblingly tapped my shoulder.

"N- Nym? C- can y- you let me by?"

I instantly knew the voice coming from behind me and stepped aside, watching Chloe creep by me. Her hand was bandaged up in several places from the incident. My stomach churned inside me as I suddenly felt sick.

"I- I'm sorry Chloe..."

Though I saw her hands tightly clench, she didn't respond or even look at me. I didn't really blame her though; she was kind to me and I hurt her. I entered the room with my head down, walking to my desk only to be stopped by the realization that my desk was gone. Looking around I saw that a single desk sat facing the wall at the front of the class. I sighed as I moseyed on to my desk and sat down.

There were people mumbling behind my back about me, but I just tried to ignore them. Yet as I sat, I felt a piece of paper hit my head then an eraser. I turned to find the culprit only to see that the entire class was cowering. All except Chloe who sat with her head down.

"Alright class- what are all of you doing?"

One of the students pointed to me looking at them.

"Nym, face the wall! Ok class let's get started."

Turning back to the wall it set in how miserable my delightful school life would be from now on. Even worse, I still had to keep up with the class while barely being able to see anything. When recess rolled around, I thought I would have a bit of time to relax. Instead, I was led to a medium sized room where a teacher would watch me for the period. Then I had lunch... which would be spent... in the same room...

"Sir? How long will I have to do this?"

He didn't answer right away, but after a minute or two he finally spoke.

"It'll probably be a few months if nothing else happens."

Months?!

Sorrow flooded me as he said it. This was my life for months! I didn't know if I could handle it all. It wasn't like the labs where I was forcibly kept alone. Here I had peers, people who I could befriend and share my time with, but it was being taken away from me for a single moment.

"I'm sorry..."

Tears started falling onto the desk beneath me.

"I promise I won't do it again- please let me try again ..."

His silence was enough to tell me that I wouldn't be getting another chance, I had ruined the only one I had. Class started up again after that, but it wasn't any different. It had become dull and unbearable.

For several days it continued like that, until one day something unexpected happened. I was alone in the bathroom crying to myself when I heard someone enter the room. As time passed, I waited for them to leave but they never did and then I heard someone in the stall nearby sobbing. While I knew it wasn't my place I wanted to see if they were ok, I wanted to help them.

Knock knock

"Hey um, are you ok in there?"

The door cracked a bit, revealing a familiar face.

"N- Nym...?"

I stumbled back a bit and turned away from Chloe as she opened the door the remainder of the way. My feet gave way as I saw the scars on her hand and I hid myself behind my arms.

"I'm so sorry Chloe, I didn't mean to, I swear."

Then I felt her arms wrap around me.

"Nym, why are you sorry? All I got was some stupid cuts, look what happened to you!"

Nervously, I let my arms fall and looked up at Chloe who was still comforting me.

"You don't hate me?"

"No! No... I'm sorry my mom told me not to be around you anymore..."

"She's probably right. You'll just get hurt again..."

She ruffled my hair.

"I won't."

I grabbed my tail and squeezed it in my arms.

"It doesn't matter anyways. It isn't like I can be around you at all."

She grabbed one of my hands.

"That's not true!"

I smiled solemnly and shook my head.

"I don't want to get in trouble."

"If they get mad, I will tell them it was my idea!"

She began dragging me off the floor and towards the exit.

"Chloe please, don't do this. You see how they treat me."

"I don't care! I know we only talked a little, but I know you aren't a mean person. Just because your body is different, it isn't fair that you have to deal with mean people."

She pulled me into the hall and walked with me back to our classroom with the few people in the halls looking on in shock. We entered our class, her scarred hand wrapped around mine. Everyone was in an uproar and the teacher moved to separate us.

"Wait please! Nym's my friend!"

A couple of people in class laughed a bit as the teacher still pulled us apart, having me hurry over to my desk against the wall. I looked to Chloe who looked distraught and mouthed that 'it's ok' as I sat down. It wasn't a lie either. She had restored a bit of the happiness I had lost, even if we weren't together. When the bell rang and it was time to go, Chloe was there waiting for me.

"Just because we can't sit together doesn't mean we can't walk together, right?"

Happily, I nodded in agreement as we moved to the school's exit. Just before the doors we separated for fear of her getting into trouble, but that was alright. Mary sat already waiting for me in the car as I walked out.

"You seem in a good mood today? Did they lift the punishment?"

"Nuh uh. It was something even better."

I watched as Chloe walked down the lot to her mom's car as we drove away to my father's house. When we arrived, I walked up to my room just like every other day and was locked inside. Emotionally exhausted, I laid back on my bed and looked to the small sheet of mostly gray paper that was pinned above my bed before dozing off.

Experiment 8 | Bullied

Before long it seemed months had passed and sure enough without much incident or argument, I was returned to my routine from before the accident. As I came into class that crisp winter morning my desk no longer sat at the front of the room. Many students murmured to one another out of concern and worry but none of that mattered. Chloe sat towards the back with several empty desks around her; a side effect of being friends with the wild animal of the school.

"I saved a seat for you."

Chloe's smile hid if she had any issue with her current situation but I still felt a bit uneasy as I glanced around at the others staring.

"I wish you wouldn't do this. I know we're friends without you standing up for me all the time."

"What sort of friend doesn't stand up for their friends?"

She turned towards one of the staring kids and stuck her tongue out at them as I sat down letting out a laugh.

I had missed being with her during class those past months but I was concerned for how it would affect her life being around me more then she already had been. It had only gotten worse since that day she reached out to me; she was even starting to get bullied because of me. All the same, class started as usual and the teacher went about teaching. For the most part it seemed the day would be uneventful at least until we got to recess.

As we left outside toward the playground, Chloe was exchanging stories from previous days at recess I had missed trying to draw out laughter from me and mostly succeeding. But before we made it I felt a sharp tug on my tail and my whole body tensed up in shock before I dropped to the ground from weak knees. I shivered lightly as I heard Chloe telling someone off.

"What are you doing?! You can't just grab her like that, she's sensitive!"

A light chuckle from a small group of people followed her comments.

"Oh yeah? That's really neat. Got any other dog facts for us?"

I let out a low growl as my nerves slowly returned to me before quickly biting my tongue and holding it in.

"She just growled!"

"She really is a dog!"

Then I heard a thud and turned my head to see one of the kids, a young boy, on the ground. Chloe had shoved him.

"Chloe stop! It isn't worth it!"

The boy grinned and started chuckling as he got to his feet.

"You should listen to your pet. After all, you wouldn't want to have the pound called would you?"

Chloe let out a faint growl mimicking me from the sounds of it causing the boy to flinch.

"Careful. I might bite you."

I grabbed hold of Chloe as the boys started to back off; she seemed to play it up by half-heartedly trying to pull away from me.

"What is going on here?" One of the teachers asked firmly; it was Miss Lyle.

Chloe turned to look with her teeth still clenched for a moment before pausing and wiping drool from her lips and stepping in front of me.

"Tommy pulled on Nym's tail."

"I did not!"

Chloe shot a glare at him and he almost tumbled back.

"Chloe, relax and take a few breaths."

Miss Lyle looked from her to Tommy then to me.

"Is this true Nym? Did this boy pull on your tail?"

I nodded hesitantly, afraid I would be in trouble again and back to being punished. She sighed and grabbed hold of Tommy's shoulder in response.

"Alright come on, you're coming to the principal's office."

"But-"

"Drop it, Tommy. This isn't the first time I have heard about you bullying people."

I blinked to myself as I watched Tommy be led away and grabbed lightly at my throat trying to catch a breath as some slight tears welled up. Chloe saw me and she quickly fell to the floor next to me, holding me close.

"It's ok, Nym, they're gone. You're going to be ok."

I sat there almost the entirety of recess with Chloe by my side, the other kids had moved on after realizing the fun was over and the teachers for the most part ignored us. That was until Miss Lyle returned without Tommy before kneeling down next to me.

"Nym dear? Are you alright?"

Still feeling a bit frightened from what had happened, I shook my head fiercely before suddenly thinking better of it and nodding.

"Did he hurt you? I don't know much about erm... well, I am sorry dear."

This time I shook my head more genuinely without much thought. It wasn't the pain from being bullied that had gotten to me after all. It was a fear that as soon as I was back to normal, it would be torn away again. As well as the relief that came with knowing it wasn't going to be. Chloe was still next to me rubbing my back gently with a worried expression.

"We should at least get you looked at, and the principal would like to hear your side of the story if that's alright? It doesn't need to be right this moment and you aren't in trouble though."

I just nodded meekly as I slowly stood up. It hadn't been that apparent while I sat, but I had at some point cut into my hands as I had done in the past. Little pools of blood sat where I had been previously and I lifted my hands to look as they shook, only now registering the pain. My eyes wandered off of them to Miss Lyle and Chloe both of whom seemed concerned as they quickly walked me to the nurse's office.

"Heavens dear, how did this happen?"

A small, tired smile formed on my face.

"I um… claws are difficult to deal with at times."

Chloe sat next to me as the nurse wrapped my hands in bandages.

"There we are, good as new."

It clearly wasn't, which made me chuckle though I thanked him all the same as I got up to go with Miss Lyle to the principal's office as Chloe went back to class. As we entered the room, I felt chills on my back and my fur stood on end before slowly sinking into a free chair. Nervously I rubbed at my hands which were itching slightly. "Nym?"

I knew the principal's voice instantly as he spoke.

"Y- yes sir?"

It was clear from his expression he had definitely taken notice of my worry.

"You aren't in trouble. You've been doing well these past months, and from what I heard from Miss Lyle here you did well today too."

I looked towards Miss Lyle who smiled softly back to me.

"So, Tommy pulled on your tail, was it?"

I nodded hesitantly.

"Now we don't know much about your condition Nym, but we would like a better understanding of you and how to help you. That being said, we would like to sit down with your father to further discuss how you are doing and things we need to look out for."

It didn't entirely set in what it was he wanted but I nodded slightly before realizing what he had said.

"He um... isn't my father sir. But well... maybe he would be fine sitting down to talk about my... condition?"

Miss Lyle and the principal shared a nervous glance not unlike I have seen before when my "father" came up in conversation. Regardless, he nodded and gestured towards the door.

"Well, that was all we wished to discuss, you may return to class now and have your father know he can expect a call from us within the next few days when you get home."

I simply nodded a bit, worried what that talk would bring me but continued back to class. Once I arrived everyone got quiet. Tommy wasn't in the room and Chloe smiled half-heartedly towards me gesturing for me to sit next to her. I did so a bit anxiously as I noticed more heavily the looks I was getting. Seemed as though school wouldn't be getting much easier after all.

Experiment 9 | Freshening Up

As the days trickled by, things didn't seem to be getting much easier. Kids at school still picked on me and Chloe almost daily. My father wasn't so thrilled to hear he had been called into the school to discuss my wellbeing. I wished they had let me bring in Mary instead even if she didn't know enough about me for what they wanted to know. She was still more of a parent then my father ever was.

Regardless, before long came the day when he would be going in with me. I awoke to find my clothes set out neatly and hurriedly put them on; it wasn't my usual uniform as we were going in on an off day. Weekends were often rough for me, just stuck in my room. I guess this was at least an excuse to get out of the house. Mary had the car out front as my father and I exited the building. I was excited to see her though I didn't want my father to know how much so. She gave a slight smile and I returned it meekly before getting into the vehicle. Just like that we were on our way to the school.

When the car pulled up to the front, I started to gather my things only to be stopped momentarily by my father.

"It would be in both of our best interests if you let me answer any questions and keep your mouth shut."

He had a bit of an intense gaze on me so I nodded quickly and took a breath before finally stepping out of the vehicle. For some reason my legs felt heavier than usual. The thought of 'why had he said that' kept repeating in my head as we entered the doors to the main lobby. It must have shown on my face how nervous I was as I received a slight thump from my father on the back to straighten up, doing so immediately. We sat there awaiting the principal to come and bring us in.

"Mr. Witherspoon?"

I glanced over to see my principal standing in the doorway with a notepad under his arm. My father stood and nodded an acknowledgement as he stuck out his hand in a formal greeting.

"It is a pleasure to finally meet you in person, I know you are a very busy man."

"Let's avoid the pleasantries, shall we?"

My father as usual was a bit gruff and hasty to get on with things as we entered the room.

"Well, sir, I know that we made a lot of exceptions for the situation of your daughter, but you see... well we want to make things a bit more approachable for someone like her."

My father gave a hefty sigh and nodded lightly.

"Then, what would you propose?"

"Well Mr. Witherspoon I was hoping we could discuss that together. With your daughter at home I am sure you have certain routines and plans on how to go about your days."

Looking at my father I could see he was a bit peeved by the comment but again he nodded.

"Well..." he took a long pause as though he had never considered what issues I may be encountering. "I suppose earplugs would be good, though we would need to have some made so if it is too much trouble I understand."

As if being bothered by the pause my principle seemed to get a bit more serious.

"Oh no, it is certainly no trouble sir, we prefer our students to be comfortable. We have also noticed your daughter tends to have trouble with her erm... claws. As you know, in a recent incident she accidentally injured a fellow student and has on multiple occasions accidentally injured herself."

My father dug out a cloth and coughed into it weakly before clearing his throat.

"I am sure we could have them trimmed."

"And how would Nym feel about that?"

He looked to me as if asking for my answer to which I turned my eyes to my father for approval which he never gave.

"Well, if it makes her safer and other students safer, I am not sure what it matters."

Yet again my principal's face showed some concern.

"It is still important to ask our kids how they are feeling sir, with all due respect."

His eyes returned to me and he nodded as though giving his own approval.

"I-I um..."

I flinched slightly expecting to get hit from my stutter and yet nothing occurred. But it was evident the principal had added something to his notes before I even continued.

"I don't like them being cut... it used to happen when-"

My eyes nervously wandered to my father who gave me a stern look as if telling me to stop there.

"They can just be sensitive I guess is all I mean, but if it would mean my friends are safer then I would be willing to try it... I guess."

The principal nodded and jotted down more notes on his paper.

"Very well then, and I suppose you have your own place where you get things like that done? A hairdresser or salon of some sort?"

"Yes."

My father said it firmly though I wasn't sure there was any such place, at least not that I had experienced. However my reaction seemed to go unnoticed by the principal as he nodded. Then after a few moments of looking over his notes he added one more thing.

"Oh yes, some students have been known to pull on your daughter's tail. Now I am not sure what exactly the standards are for such a thing, but I think it would be wise to invest in longer skirts for her uniform she could hide her tail under."

Father's eyes narrowed and he looked almost angry.

"So, it's my daughter's fault that little bratty children don't know to leave young ladies alone?"

My fur stood on end and I felt a shiver as he said it. In all my time with my father I hadn't heard him refer to me in such a manner.

"No Mr. Witherspoon, that is not at all what I was trying to say. I just meant it would likely be simpler for your daughter if it was out of reach from the offending children."

Still a bit stunned I heard a gruff breath from my father as he stood from where he had been sitting.

"Well, I will do just that. But if I hear of further incidents against my daughter, I assure you that you will be hearing from me."

"Of course, sir, I understand your frustrations and concerns. We will be watching over her in our care though, you have nothing to worry about."

My father let out a low annoyed chuckle and grabbed hold of my hand lighter than he ever had.

"Come now, we have some stuff to do before Monday rolls around Nym."

I almost couldn't help but smile as I got up to follow him to the door. He continued like that to the car. Then as we sat and buckled up, he released my hand and brushed his against his cloth he carried. The ride home was quiet otherwise; I had a small grin on my face for most of it. As we drove up to the house I began to wonder what might be happening to me after all of that, but I tried to shake off the thought as we walked up the steps. Just before we entered, my father turned to Mary.

"Go into town and pick up these things for Nym, would you?"

Mary looked down at a small list he gave her with confusion painted across her face though she nodded and went about it anyway. Afterwards, we finally entered the house and for once I wasn't immediately returned to my room and was instead led to my father's study.

I had been in it once before but never took the time to look around. There were many papers strewn about and tons of books, many with words I didn't even know written on them. Pictures of sketches hung above the desk my father used for work and a small skeleton of someone like me sat in a case; it was Subject 16.

"Take a seat here Nym."

My father gestured to a chair I had seen several times in the past and suddenly I felt sick.

"P- please father I'll do whatever you want me to, just don't make m-"

Smack

I felt his hand hit hard against my cheek before nodding a horrible acceptance and finding my way to the seat.

"Much easier when you cooperate isn't it?"

With that a strap tightened around one arm, then another, then around my forehead followed by my legs. It had been years since I had ever been put like this. When

I still was young and wild and froth with anger I was put here for experimentation. My heart pounded in my chest awaiting whatever needle or knife was about to make contact with my skin. But instead I felt one of my hands being lifted into my fathers.

"Hold still."

I looked up to him.

"What are you going t-"

Snap

A sharp pain ran through one of my fingers and I let out a shrill scream as my whole body shook and shivered. My eyes wandered down to my hand where my father was preparing to cut off another of my claws.

"Wait wait wait-!"

Snap

Another pain shot through me and I began to sob lightly.

"P- please father-"

Snap snap snap

I felt almost dizzy as he finished his handy work. Little droplets of blood ran off my fingertips. I didn't even feel the pain anymore as the tears continued running down my cheeks. I tried to focus on my father with my eyes but it was hazy. Just then I could hear a gasp from the other side of the room and for a moment glimpsed Mary before dozing into unconsciousness.

Experiment 10 | Aftermath

When morning came, a knock came with it and slowly I found myself sitting up in bed. My hands were aching and I was hesitant to see what state they were in at the moment. So instead I looked to the door to see who would enter, a bit fearful it would be my father. Fortunately it was Mary who peeked her head in. She dropped a bag on the ground and came over to my bedside.

"Hey sweetie."

Her faint smile didn't hide her concern for me nor did the soft tone of her voice. Her eyes seemed to wander down to where my hands sat.

"How are you feeling?"

"I'm doing ok I guess. My hands though…"

Mary tried to force a warmer smile while slowly moving to take my hands as I winced lightly finally letting myself look at my hands. They were bandaged diligently around the fingers and shook weakly against my will.

After a moment I took a breath before continuing my answer.

"Will my hands be ok? They hurt Miss Mary."

"Honestly? I'm not sure. We've never seen someone like you Nym, you're special."

"I'm a freak..."

I mumbled it quietly as tears began welling in the corners of my eyes. Mary brought a hand to my cheek and lightly caressed it.

"You are not a freak. Maybe you are a bit different then most kids your age, but that's ok Nym. No one needs you to be anyone other than you."

I held my hands up shakily.

"Tell that to my father."

Her frown showed she didn't disagree and instead of answering right away she gave me a hug then pulled away after a moment longer.

"I'm sorry. You're right. What he did to you isn't right, none of this has been."

I sniffled and rubbed at my eyes lightly with the backs of my hands.

"What should I even do? Will he cut off my tail next... ? My ears...?"

"No. No he wouldn't do that."

"He said I wasn't successful… maybe he'll just put me in a box like some of the others…"

Firm hands landed on my shoulders and I looked up at Mary.

"I would never let that happen to you Nym. You are a good kid and nothing about how your body is or what you are is going to change that."

I nodded meekly and took a deep breath.

"What um… what did my father have you getting earlier?"

She sighed and smiled before getting up from the bedside and going over the bag she had set down when she came in. After opening it she began digging around until she produced several lengthy skirts and a crimson hat that seemed a bit poofy.

"Things that your father had me buy for you. I would guess because of your talk with the school."

I nodded as I got out of bed and walked over to pick up the hat only to stop before touching it for fear of it hurting my hand.

"Yeah… they want me to hide my ears and tail to get bullied less I guess."

She smiled to me softly as she picked up the hat and slowly adjusted it on my head. It felt incredibly stuffy on my ears and everything seemed a bit quieter.

"For what it's worth I think it suits you."

She moved over to my mirror and turned it so I could get a look at myself. As I stood there staring back at the person on the other side of the glass I felt almost dazed. For a moment if I ignored the bandages on my hands and held my tail still I could almost mistake myself for a normal young girl. I smiled meekly and let out a sad giggle before slowly raising my hand to my head pulling the hat off, wincing as I did so. There I was again, the real me.

"Do you think I will always have to hide Miss Mary?"

I looked at her expectedly still holding the hat in my hand.

"I hope not sweetie, but only time will tell."

A smile formed on my face again as I nodded thankful for her honesty.

"I think I'm going to lay back down for a bit to rest. It was a long day."

"Day? Nym it's Sunday."

"O- oh"

My gaze returned to my hands and I sighed.

"So I guess this won't be healed by the time school starts on Monday then?"

Mary let out a brief laughter and nodded.

"What's so funny, Miss Mary?"

"Nothing, it's just that most kids don't care for school that much and here you are, even with everything that's happened and all they are making you do, still excited."

"Honestly... I just want to see Chloe."

She smiled and softly pat the top of my head.

"I am glad you were able to make a friend at school. Everything is going well with her?"

"Yeah, it is. Her um... her hand healed a bit ago. If it weren't for the... the scar you could hardly know she was hurt."

"You know it really wasn't your fault Nym?"

"It sure feels like it was..."

Mary sighed and had me look her in the eyes.

"You're young Nym, you haven't had time to learn all about yourself much less the things most kids have to deal with at your age. It was a brief moment and an accident. If your friend forgives you and she's ok then that's that."

I nodded then shook off her gaze.

"I think I am going to rest now if that's ok?"

She gave a warm smile and stood up to go to the door before stopping in the doorway.

"If you need anything at all come find me or just call for me."

With that I was alone in my room again. After I was sure she was away I got up and went to my bag for school, pouring out the supplies from inside it. I moved to pick up a pencil a bit timidly but quickly dropped it. My hand shook and ached. Then I took a breath before again going to pick it up, this time trying to ignore the pain. Next I found my notebook and tried to open it which took several tries.

My hand shook worse as I pressed my pencil to the paper, trying to ignore it as I went to write. As suspected it wasn't easy and before long the pencil fell from my hand as pain shot up it. I moved to close the notebook with a long sigh but soon gave up in favor of returning to bed. Tears began forming in my eyes again and streaming down, starting to doze off. Hopefully tomorrow will be a better day.

Experiment 11 | Anxieties

The next day came along all too quickly as I rolled out of bed. My hands still ached as I lifted myself off the floor. I glanced around the room to my things still strewn about the room and sighed as I began to put it all back into my bag. Just then, a light tapping came at my door.

"May I come in?"

Mary's voice slipped through the door and after a second I replied.

"Yes, thanks for asking."

She entered and walked over to where I was sitting gathering up things.

"Sorry, I had a bit of a moment last night after you stepped out..."

"It's alright Nym, let me help you with that."

Not long after she knelt down to help me with my bag, it was packed up once more. Afterwards, I got up to start getting ready for my day but my hands were already shaking rather violently from pain as I grabbed my hat. I held them against each other trying to stop their shaking and took a breath. Just as I did so Mary came over and started unwrapping the bandages on my fingers.

I didn't think they looked infected, but they didn't look especially well either. Each finger looked darkened and bruised at the tips, my claws now clearly absent from them minus small jagged bits that had been patched with something. Almost as quickly as the thoughts crossed my mind, Miss Mary had already started rewrapping my fingers with new, clean bandages. She smiled warmly at me and turned to pick up something she had brought with her I hadn't seen before.

"Here, these should help at least hide the bandages while you're at class."

She held out a pair of dark maroon gloves.

"My father thought I should hide it I guess?"

"No. I thought with everything you had going on people knowing you were hurt would just make things worse for you."

A faint smile formed on my face as I took the gloves from her with a nod. Then, somewhat painfully, I slipped them over my hands. Finally I was ready for my day even if I felt numb and dull from all the covering up. But before we left the house I realized I would need to get breakfast.

Soon after I finished my food, I was up and to the car on my way to school. As we rode towards it we sat somewhat quietly, I think we both were still considering the weekend we had been through. Before long I found myself shaken from my thoughts by a hand on my shoulder.

"We're here Nym."

I nodded and took a deep breath.

"Ok... I'm going then, wish me luck."

I put on a quick smile and grabbed my bag as I stepped out of the car mentally preparing myself for what was likely a rough day. Almost as though to confirm my suspicion a teacher informed me hats were against dress code and it would need to be removed indoors. Hesitantly, I pulled the hat off and continued to my classroom.

As I went down the hall, I could tell people thought I looked out of place and by the time I found my way to my desk many eyes had passed over me. I nearly went to scratch at myself in nerves before remembering the recent state of my claws and stopping myself. But then there was Chloe waiting for me as I sat down greeting me with a smile.

"Hey! I see you got some new fashion!"

I laughed anxiously but nodded.

"Y- yeah something like that."

Her face told me rather quickly that she wasn't convinced.

"What's wrong?"

"Nothing."

"Nym. I know we only see each other at school, but I know you are upset about something. Does it have to do with the new clothes?"

"No. I- it's fine for real."

Chloe reached over to softly rest her hand on mine in a form of comfort causing me to quickly pull away and gasp faintly in pain.

"What happened to your hand?"

"I said it's fine. Please."

Though she still didn't seem convinced she smiled weakly and nodded.

"Ok, fine. But tell me later about it."

I nodded back not really thinking much of it as class started. As per usual it was boring and I didn't really need to be taught a lot of it. At some point I must've dozed off because the teacher called on me and I found myself sitting up with many eyes on me.

"Y- yes ma'am?"

"Nym, come to the front here and write this bit here for us please."

"I uh…" my eyes flickered about "I don't think that's a very good idea right now."

Looking a bit peeved, the teacher nodded and moved on to someone else for the time being. Nonetheless a few minutes later she returned to me and I was made to come up to the front. As I did so I felt almost light headed and dizzy. Taking a red marker from the tray I raised it up to start answering the problem on the board only for my hand to shake. After a shaky start it seemed to look fine enough until the marker slipped from my hand.

Instinctually, I quickly went to catch it and bumped my fingers on the ground causing a sharp piercing pain to shoot up them and a yelp to come from my mouth. My hand went to cover the noise quickly, but sadly not quickly enough. I looked around the class to see every-one staring at me and felt my cheeks glowing a bit.

"S- sorry ma'am… I- I'll just um…"

Timidly I went to head back to my desk, hanging my head low as I did so. Small giggling could be heard from here and there in the classroom though the teacher and Chloe seemed less amused. As I took my seat the teacher called out for everyone to be quiet and continued the lesson. Chloe nudged me to get my attention as the teacher went back to her lesson.

"Hey are you ok?"

My hands were still shaking and I decided to lay down my head to ignore her and the others.

"Nym, can you talk to me, please? I'm worried about you."

Finally yielding I slowly sat up and turned to her.

"I just hurt my hands a little is all. They'll be fine."

"You did or...?"

I sighed and turned away from her again.

"Who did it?"

"Just leave it."

She slowly reached over to my hand and I went to pull it away before stopping at the memory of what happened last time I pulled away from her. As she held my hand lightly she pulled at the glove to remove it. It stung as it finally gave free and revealed the bandaged fingers underneath.

"Oh Nym... what did they do to you?"

"The school... They suggested to my father that I should adjust to blend in and be more normal so that

I am less of a target. I got a hat… and a long skirt… and…"

"H- he didn't…"

Again I pulled away my hand but nodded a confirmation.

"That isn't right… it's a part of you!"

Chloe's uproar caught the attention of several people in class including the teacher who came to stand over us.

"Is there a problem over here?"

Her eyes wandered down to my uncovered hand and her face looked a bit pale.

"Take her to the nurses office."

"No, ma'am, it's ok it isn't fresh it's from-"

Again I covered my mouth and looked downward away from the teacher.

"What is it, Nym? How did this happen?"

"It's fine, my claws just needed a trim…"

Our teacher's eyes widened a bit before looking about the class and encouraging everyone to get back to work before returning to me.

"See me after class."

Experiment 12 | Teacher Conference

"**N**ym? I need you to talk to me, ok?"

I held my hands quivering in my lap as I sat across from Ms. Margaret. It wasn't entirely clear what it was she wanted me to say, but as I caught a glance of her looking at my hands I started to suspect what this was about.

"About what, Miss?"

She let out a sigh and turned to type something on her computer.

"What're you typing?"

"Nothing you need to worry about, Nym."

She turned back to me and smiled meekly.

"Now, tell me again how your hands got like this?"

I let my feet kick lightly while looking at the floor shrugging as I did so.

"Like I said Miss. They needed a trim, and the principal talked to my father about it."

"Right... Well, they look pretty bad, though I won't pretend to know how this works for you. Would you be ok if we took a walk to the nurse's office to have those looked at?"

Slowly I shook my head fearful of what might come of it.

"I said I'm fine, Miss. Honest."

My gaze finally lifted off the floor back to her.

"Let's just have them take a look anyways, what could it hurt?"

As we walked down the hallway towards the nurse's office I quickly realized I wasn't going to be able to talk my way out of this. My hand lightly tapped on my leg wishing I could scratch at it but to no avail. Then we arrived at the office and entered. I nervously sat in one of the chairs waiting for what would come next while Ms. Margaret gave a reassuring smile. Just then the nurse entered the room and went to check his computer before turning to me.

"So, what appears to be the problem tod-"

It was clear from his pause that he had taken note of the problem in question. He leaned down by me and smiled warmly.

"Is it ok if I look? I promise I will be gentle."

I nodded hesitantly, inviting him to investigate my wounds. After a moment he did just that unwrapping each finger carefully while trying to hide a grimace through each one he revealed. It was clear he wasn't entirely sure what he was working with, but another thing was clear too; he knew I was hurting.

"Alright Nym... how was it you got these?"

My head hung low but before long I responded all the same.

"M- my father... h- he was told that I should..."

Tears started rolling down my cheeks and quickly I went to rub at them to go away.

"And were you alright with this?"

Moments passed before I ended up uncertainly shaking my head.

"N- no... t- they were mine... it was part of me..."

Ms. Margaret and the nurse exchanged a concerned glance as my eyes drifted down to my shaking hands while sobs took my voice. After the nurse wrapped my hands, they let me sit for a good while longer before Ms. Margaret had to step back to class while I gathered myself. When that time came I looked over to the nurse who simply smiled and gave me a lollipop. I unwrapped it carefully before putting it in my mouth; the taste on its own nearly caused new tears.

"You're a tough kid you know?"

I nodded meekly.

"I'm supposed to be."

His face curled into a frown briefly before he smiled again.

"Well if you like you can head back to class, or you can stay here a bit longer if you don't feel up to it just yet."

"I'll be fine I think, thank you."

He gave a nod and waved a hand as if to say farewell to which I got up and headed out of the room. The walk back to class felt slow and uneasy. What would happen now after this? Would I be alright? Those cloudy thoughts stormed me as I walked along until coming up to the door of the classroom. There I stood for a short bit not sure that I wanted to go in just yet before entering the room.

Everyone there including the teacher looked to me. I felt so self-conscious as I moseyed on over to where my desk was. My hands ached more than they had earlier and I felt dizzy. It was getting hard to breathe. My heart felt like it was beating in my ears. Finally, I made it to my desk and slumped into it. My eyes danced around in front of me; why did it seem like I was still being stared at? Suddenly I felt a hand on my shoulder and I nearly fell from my chair.

"Nym? Are you ok?"

After a breath or two I glanced around the room; no one was watching. Still my breathing felt heavy as I turned to find whoever the hand belonged to.

"C- Chloe? Yeah. Yeah, I'm ok."

"What did the teacher need you for?"

"I don't know... they just wanted to talk."

"What about?"

I was starting to get irritated at her prying and I sighed in frustration as I laid my head down on my desk.

"Just leave it, Chloe."

Her hand lightly found its way to my back and began rubbing it softly.

"It'll be ok Nym, whatever it is."

As I laid there on my desk I couldn't help but feel she was mistaken. It didn't feel like it would be fine. I had messed up badly and it was surely going to come back to bite me. My head turned slightly to catch a look at the clock on the wall before I let out another sigh. Why did time move so slow when so much was going on.

I watched the time tick by as it grew ever closer to my freedom and just before class was over, I placed my hat over my ears. It was true that the hat helped muffle the sound, but distinctly the bell still rang loudly in my ears. I quickly got to my feet and gathered my things trying to ignore everyone and everything going on around me as I headed for the door. Despite the muffled nature of my hearing, I still heard the murmurs and rumoring of many people as I went.

Someone yelled after me but I didn't hear what they were saying as I stepped out of the front door of the school. Once I was in the car with Miss Mary, my breathing finally slowed a bit but the ringing remained a few moments longer and my heart hadn't quieted.

"Are you ok?"

Hurriedly I nodded not wanting them to think anything was wrong; not convincing anyone.

"What happened Nym? Did someone bully you again?"

My head hung low and I murmured something to myself.

"What was that?"

"M- my father... he bullied me... and now everyone is worried about me and saying stuff and I don't know what I did and I tried really hard to hide it but it didn't work, none of it worked..."

Mary frowned at me as I realized I had misspoken. It was too late though and as she shifted the car into drive, I could already tell it was going to be a quiet ride home.

Experiment 13 | Sickly

When we pulled up to the house Mary just sat there quietly in the car as if wanting to say something. Before she said anything though she got out of the car and waved for me to follow. We walked up the steps in silence and into the house. With a soft yet melancholic smile Mary sent me along to my room. Once I got inside my room I found my way to my bed and laid down for a bit.

While laying there on my bed thinking back on my day, I began to hear yelling from outside. For a short while I listened to the muffled shouts before finally slipping off my hat to listen a little better. Even without the hat it was somewhat difficult to listen but as I focused I started to make out words.

"-is just a child! Your child!"

"That creature is going to ruin everything!"

"Sir, you can't honestly expect her to take that blame?!"

"And why not...?!"

A few moments passed without me hearing anything so I decided to get closer to hopefully listen clearer. Slowly I creeped towards the door opening it and tiptoeing down towards the voices. As they came into clear earshot I slid down to sit on the stairs and listen to hear what Mary was saying now.

"-died for this."

"That wasn't part of the plan."

"Yes well, how well is that going for you?"

"If it weren't for that useless animal, it could have changed the world."

"Oh boo-hoo, your little experiment didn't work out. Well, who cares. You still have a kid to take care of. What does torturing her accomplish?"

"You know what, I don't need this, get out!"

"One day your behavior will come back to haunt you."

"I said out!"

Smash

Thump

The sounds echoed in my ears as I quickly got to my feet, hurrying to the other room to see what had happened. When I arrived there were shards of glass and trickling liquid all over one section of the floor. Mary was half obscured from view behind my father's desk with his feet barely sticking out past it. As if by instinct, my hand went to my chest feeling my heart pounding.

"W- what happened?"

Mary's eyes fraught with fear and worry turned their attention to me, widening as they did so.

"Nym, you're supposed to be in your room, why aren't you in your room?"

I stumbled back a few steps before hesitantly walking over to where my father was lying. At first glance it didn't seem as though anything should be wrong but then I noticed his breathing was raspy.

"What happened?"

The words came out clearer a second time, more determined to find an answer.

"He was furious and threw his glass then collapsed while coughing... your father is sick Nym."

As usual she didn't pull any punches when it came to informing me of things. I meekly leaned down over my father and looked him over. I wasn't sure why, but it hurt to see him like that. Tears were welling up but I quickly wiped them knowing he didn't like it when I cried.

"Will he be ok?"

She didn't reply and instead walked over to her bag producing a phone from it and calling someone or another. In another 15 minutes I could hear sirens outside blaring so loudly I had to cover my ears. While they came in and removed my father from the room I sat there, ears still covered, breathing heavily on the floor. Mary was caught up getting asked things by some of the people that had arrived.

Before long the sirens of the vehicle outside vanished and I was left there on the floor in a mostly quiet house. A light tapping came at the office's entrance and I looked up to find Mary in the doorway. She came over and sat down next to me as I wiped more tears from my eyes. It was quiet like that for a short time until I finally got the courage to speak up.

"Is he gonna die? Am I gonna be alone?"

"Nym..."

She wrapped an arm around me and gave me a squeeze.

"He is likely going to be fine. And even if he wasn't you wouldn't be alone you know."

Worriedly, I looked up to her.

"I wouldn't...?"

"No Nym, I would still be here after all."

She smiled to me and kissed the top of my head lightly.

"Um... Miss Mary... can I ask you something?"

"Of course?"

"I- is my mom… dead because of me?"

From her expression I could see she wasn't fully expecting the question and as it twisted around I could tell she was struggling to think of an answer. She let out a soft sigh before talking.

"Well… no, not exactly."

"What do you mean?"

"I guess that it wasn't really your fault."

"But she did die from me?"

"When you were born Nym… well… leading up to it your mother and father were very happy. Everything was going right; the experiment, the child, their relationship. Everything was perfect."

I shuffled in place nervously.

"W- what happened?"

"Your mother got very sick towards the end of everything. At first the doctors couldn't figure out why she was feeling that way, but then it became apparent that it was linked to the child she was carrying."

"I made my mother sick?"

"No dear… your father made your mother sick. They had done a lot to make sure you would be safe and that you would be born into this world, they just hadn't done enough for your mother. In the end her body couldn't handle the stress of it and it started to give out on her. She passed shortly after you were born."

My head felt woozy as I listened to her speak and I started to feel almost sickly.

"Is that why my father hates me...?"

She let out a sigh before starting to get to her feet.

"Come on. Let's go get you some dinner, alright?"

"You didn't answer me..."

Again she sighed as she helped me off the ground and started to walk me to the kitchen with her. Somehow as she started to cook I felt as though I wouldn't be getting an answer that evening. In the end, I didn't.

Experiment 14 | Interrogation

As the evening progressed I began worrying as to what would happen to me. It wasn't as though a kid like me would be wanted by many people. Maybe I would end up in an orphanage… or worse, another lab. Shaking off the thought, I walked over to my bag from school and pulled out my homework sitting to complete it. 'Just have to focus on school,' I told myself as I copied down the words from the paper. Before I knew it I found myself dozing off at my desk.

Knock knock

Light rapping came at my door and I groggily sat up still at my desk from the night before. Slowly, I got up and went over to the door as it cracked open slightly. There stood Mary, with a man and a woman I didn't know behind her.

"Sorry, did I wake you?"

"Y- yeah… it's fine I have school soon anyways."

My gaze must have been noticed by Mary towards those behind her.

"Oh. These nice people here are wanting to discuss some things with you about your time living here and living with your father."

"A- are they going to take me away from him...?"

Anxiously, my eyes wandered to the ground and I squeezed lightly the side of my skirt with my hand still aching a bit from the trimming. I could see out of the corner of my eyes that someone had knelt down in front of me causing me to glance up. It was the lady who had been behind Mary, she had a soft smile on her face.

"Hi there, are you Nym?"

I nodded still nervous.

"I'm Janie and this is Baxter, here."

She gestured over to the guy then continued.

"We are here to ask you some questions about your dad and how you like living here."

"It's fine."

I said it firmly but couldn't help but let a quiver slip into my words.

"Nym, you can be honest with us. We are just here to help you if you let us."

I bit my lip and again looked away from her.

"How did you get these?"

She pointed to my bandaged hands and I self-consciously hid them.

"J- just needed a trim is all."

"That looks like more than a trim Nym. Are you alright?"

"It stung a bit is all…"

"Stung? Could you describe how it felt?"

My eyes looked back to her then to her friend before lastly lingering on Mary.

"D- did you call them?"

"I didn't, no."

"Then…"

Janie placed her hand on my shoulder trying to get my attention again.

"Look, let's go downstairs and take a seat then we can discuss all of this a bit more. Are you alright with that Nym?"

I nodded timidly as they all went to go down the stairs. Meekly, I followed until I got to the bottom. There I stood a moment looking between the door outside and the hallway that the others had started down. This was it; I could just run here… they wouldn't catch me…

"Nym?"

I turned to look back down the hallway and Mary was there looking nervously between me and the door. I quickly followed down the hallway towards the sitting room where we all sat to talk. It was only my second time having sat in that room, it always felt wrong being there.

"Alright then. Tell us again about how you felt when your hands... well...?"

Her look was telling me I couldn't get out of answering so after a moment I did.

"I- it hurt a lot... I um... passed out."

Her friend's brows furrowed as he jotted down something in a notebook he carried.

"What did he write?"

"No worries Nym. Anyways, we saw your room was somewhat scarce compared to the rest of the home, not a fan of a cluttered room?"

"Y- yeah. Prefer one more like mine."

Again the friend wrote something down.

"W- what did he write now?"

"It's ok, let's continue. So what about other things? Do you eat well?"

"I get fed yeah."

"Get fed? Interesting phrasing."

Was it interesting? What had I said that time?

"I um... yeah... I am fed, that's what you asked yeah?"

More scribbling in the notebook.

"And you ate with your dad?"

"F- for breakfast, yes. Father is a busy man."

"Busy? Would you say he doesn't give you enough attention?"

"No, no... I mean... he gives me plenty enough I think?"

"You don't sound so sure."

I sat there holding the side of the chair tightly, causing my hands to shake. My eyes went to Mary and I could feel my breathing growing heavy. As it did I looked back to Janie while trying to take a deep breath. It wasn't helping. Suddenly I felt the urge to run out of the room.

"Are you alright?"

She scooted a bit closer looking concerned.

"You need to breathe Nym. Deep breaths in and out."

She made an attempt to mimic what she was telling me to do and I did my best to follow. After a short while I felt my heart slow its pace back to where it started and could breathe again. Soon, I was curled up in the chair and was trying not to look at anyone.

"It's alright. Some people have anxiety, especially when they've been through stuff like-"

"There isn't anything wrong! I haven't been through anything!"

I cut her off and held my hands over my ears desperate not to think about what she was saying. No luck. Those thoughts kept swarming in my mind.

"Maybe it would be better if we came back in a bit?"

I looked up and saw Mary nod while Janie flashed a final smile before getting up to head out of the room. Afterward, Mary took a seat next to me sighing until she turned to face me with a soft look. My shaking hadn't stopped and my nerves were still running high but I felt a bit better just alone there with her then.

"C- can I go to school now...?"

Her smile faded slightly though she nodded.

"I can talk with them about coming back after, but you will likely be a bit late. It's alright to stay home if you need to for today."

I shook my head slowly which led to her getting up and heading out of the room. Sluggishly, I went about my usual morning routine and got ready for the day of school that was ahead of me. Before long we were in the car heading that way with all the thoughts and questions lingering in my head. It was going to be a long day.

Experiment 15 | Dazed

When we arrived at school it had been nearly two hours since class had started. Surprisingly, Mary parked the car and walked with me inside. It was mostly empty in the halls as she walked me into the office to explain why I was late and to get me a note for when I eventually headed to class. My feet dragged along while I slowly moseyed towards my classroom after she waved me off, nervous of the day ahead and lost in thought of everything that had happened.

The door to the room creaked slightly as I pulled it open to slip inside; the teacher was staring at me along with most of the class. I hurriedly went to set my note on the desk at the front of the room before going to take my seat. There were murmurs all around me about all sorts of things, but most of it passed over me as if I weren't really hearing it at all. It wasn't until I felt a familiar hand on my shoulder that I finally snapped back to where I was and away from that far off place in my mind.

"Are you ok?"

"Y- yeah… no… I don't know…"

Chloe's face was a mix of confusion and concern and she let out a soft sigh before smiling faintly. I tried to return the smile but it didn't hold long until my melancholy took me once more. She glanced toward the teacher at the front of class and leaned over to whisper to me.

"Did something happen at home?"

I slowly nodded before resting a hand on the side of my head scratching at it. How so much could happen in a single day was beyond me at the time. At the moment I still wasn't sure how to feel about what was going on.

"Did someone hurt you?"

It was a good question, one which I didn't have a direct answer for.

"It's just… a lot happened…"

She nodded and stole another glance to the front of the class. When she didn't continue speaking, I stole a glance too and saw that the teacher was staring at us. I slowly looked away and hid my face halfway behind my hand. My head was aching lightly and my eyes stung for some reason unknown to me. What was this feeling? It felt like when I was sad but also twinged with anger or disappointment...

Murmuring voices gathered again and I covered my ears to block them out before a sharp crack against my desk knocked me out of my thoughts again. I sat up quickly, nearly falling out of my chair as I looked around the room then to the teacher standing over me with her ruler.

"Please pay attention Nym."

I nodded, half-aware of my surroundings and leaned forward looking down to my notebook I didn't remember pulling from my bag. Until lunch, my class continued in much of the same manner. Randomly I would find myself missing from the room off in my mind either thinking of things that have happened or things that could. When lunch came, the bell's shrill ring woke me from my trance and I quickly shuffled to my feet with Chloe. As we walked down the hall to the cafeteria I could feel her worried gaze following me from time to time. Then when we sat to eat I felt it constantly. I couldn't blame her though even I knew I was in rough shape as I sat picking at my food only eating bits here and there. Finally she spoke up and asked again.

"What happened?"

Pretending not to hear it I looked away from Chloe. "Nym. I know you can hear me; you have amazing hearing."

I felt my cheeks grow redder at the sudden compliment and for a moment forgot what I was worrying about until it rushed back.

"I don't know if I'll have a home much longer..."

Chloe's face was clearly trying to hide her panic at the statement though was doing a poor job of it.

"What do you mean?"

"M- my dad is sick and some weird people came to ask me all sorts of questions."

"What sort of questions?"

Thinking back on it, my breath started to grow heavy like it had several times before, but this time I remembered what I had been told and slowly began taking breaths slowly and deeply. Noticing this Chloe reached out and rested a hand on my arm reassuringly.

"T- thanks"

My words were shaky with my breath but Chloe smiled warmly at me.

"Always, what are friends for anyways?"

I smiled back genuinely and let out a sigh.

"My dad is dying... and I don't know where I am going to end up or if anyone else will want me."

Tears started to form as I finally said it. Telling her made it feel even more real then it had earlier that day. Almost as though I was speaking it into solidity. Chloe's eyes grew a bit as I said it and seeing my tears she started tearing up before bringing me into a hug.

"I- I don't know what to say Nym... I'm so sorry..."

"It's ok... not like I can do anything about it."

She nodded in understanding before trying to force a smile.

"And what about Mary? Can she take you in?"

Suddenly my foggy thoughts became a bit clearer. Why hadn't I thought about that...

"I... I don't know? I just thought... maybe?" Hopefully.

Another ring of the bell told us lunch time was over and with a bit of hesitancy I headed back towards the classroom. Some of the kids in front of Chloe and I were looking back to us while whispering to each other which I tried to ignore. Soon enough we were back at our desks and back to working on mind-numbing assignments.

Within the routine of it all I found myself back in my own brain thinking of all the stuff that could happen. What if Mary didn't want me and was just doing all this because she was getting paid...? What if my dad got better...? Would things go back to normal then...? What even is normal...?

While the thoughts raced the time seemed to slow. Every so often when I felt it had been awhile I would glance at the clock; seconds seemed to tick by slower and slower as I watched it. My hand went up to scratch at myself again. It was becoming a habit. Again, I took a few breaths and looked around the room. It all felt so slow.

After what felt like ages the final bell rang and we were released. Slowly I got up with Chloe holding onto me loosely. She smiled meekly at me and I returned it while the panic of going home slowly set in. I kept breathing as steadily as I could but I could tell my heart was starting to pound in my chest.

As we came to the door, Chloe finally released me before smiling once more and heading out so her mom didn't know we were still hanging out. What about Chloe and school? Would I even be here? Would I even have her in my life after all of this? What if they took me to some far-off orphanage in some far-off place and I never saw anyone I knew ever again?

I stood in the doorway of the front of the school for a while thinking about that until I saw Mary pull up. I didn't want to go back now, more than maybe ever. In a moment I made a decision and started walking towards Mary's car then past it and then I picked up the pace before running. I could hear Mary calling after me but I tried not to listen as it faded behind me.

Experiment 16 | She's a Little Runaway

By the time I stopped running my legs were tired and my breathing was raspy. After a moment of catching my breath, I slowly slumped down to the ground before looking around me to see where I ended up. It wasn't so busy where I was and there were only a handful of buildings around. It didn't take long to notice I was entirely lost and had never been there before.

While I finished resting, I remembered my hat in my bag and slipped out to put it on thinking it would make me stand out less. My hands brushed myself off as I stood before continuing down the road I was on. As I went along, I kept glancing around at the people who looked down to me as I walked. Taking a deep breath and softly scratching at my arm, the realization of what I did set in.

There was a sick feeling in the pit of my stomach. I didn't know where I was even going or where I would end up after all of this. I put myself in the place I was worried about ending up. A bench came into view on the path and I sat down, looking down into my bag with a frown. *"At least I did this myself,"* I had thought while sitting there digging around for something to do. Shortly thereafter, I retrieved a notebook along with my red coloring supplies and began to draw.

I wasn't entirely sure how much time had passed when my stomach growled alerting me to my hunger. My eyes wandered to the places around me as my hand rested lightly on my stomach. Taking a breath, I slid my stuff back into my bag before walking over to what I thought might be a restaurant unless my sense of smell was betraying me. When I arrived at the door I peaked in through the window and saw that people were eating pizza inside. Drool rolled down from my mouth as I took in the smell again and quickly wiped it away.

"Excuse us, little girl."

I flinched at the words and turned to see a couple of people standing behind me.

"Sorry, we just needed the door."

They went to open the door as the person with them looked at me a bit longer.

"Are you lost? Who are you here with?"

Nervously, I looked away from them and took a few

steps back as the person kneeled down to eye level with me.

"It's alright. Look how about you just go wait inside for your parents and we can have them give them a call ... Do you know their numbers?"

I turned to hurry off only to stop at another growl from my stomach. I stood there shaking lightly. What was I doing?

"Hey, ok, we won't do that..."

I could feel them coming up closer behind me.

"How about you at least come in and we can get you some food. It's a bit chilly out here anyways."

I looked back and saw that they had put their hand out. I knew I wasn't supposed to trust strangers but my hunger was winning and I meekly nodded as I went with them inside. We sat quietly until one of them spoke up.

"So um... what sort of pizza do you like?"

Finally, I looked at her directly.

"I... I guess pepperoni?"

She nodded and turned to mutter something to her friend. If I hadn't been wearing my hat I could likely have heard it. It always made me nervous when I couldn't hear what was going on. After a person came along, she told them what we wanted and walked off. Her gaze returned to me with a weak smile.

"So, what's your name?"

"It's Nym…"

"Nym? That's a nice name."

"Thank you…"

The two of them stole a glance at each other and laughed lightly.

"Very polite. Though you go to that fancy school down the road right?"

"I- No!"

People around us were looking over at our table and I slumped down into my chair.

"S- sorry."

The two of them took a worried glance at each other before looking back at me.

"It's ok Nym. You don't have to talk about it if you don't want to."

I nodded meekly as one of them got up to walk off towards the bathroom. As they were away, it was quiet again and before long we had the food in front of us. While we started eating she finally returned to the table and sat down. Her smile remained but it seemed weaker somehow though I shrugged it off in favor of eating.

As we got close to finishing the food, I felt a bit more at ease and my thoughts seemed a lot clearer. My gaze went back to the lady who had asked about my school and went to answer before remembering I hadn't asked her name.

"Oh um... sorry but, what was your name?"

She smiled warmly and gestured to the person with her.

"This is Charlie and I'm Niko."

I nodded then continued.

"I... do go to that school, yeah."

She nodded, looking a bit serious.

"Alright and are you in trouble? Did you get lost on the way home? Or did you maybe run away from home or something?"

I nervously scratched at the edge of my hat.

"Sorry, it's just a bit strange for someone as young as you to be out at this hour by yourself. Your family is probably worried."

I shook my head and frowned; no one was worried about me and no one was going to be waiting for me back home.

"I'm alone now I think..."

"Oh come now, I'm sure there is somebody. Do you have any family?"

"My um... father is dying."

At the silence I glanced up; both of them were looking at me with pity in their eyes.

"It's fine. He was a bad dad anyways."

"I see… well what about mom?"

"Died when I was born."

Both of them frowned deeply.

"Oh… sorry… any other family?"

I shook my head timidly.

"None alive that I know of."

Just then, I heard the shuffling of several people entering the place and turned slightly in my chair to see what was going on. There stood two people in uniforms I felt I had seen somewhere. Suddenly all of my nerves came rushing back.

"I- I have to get going now."

Quickly, I grabbed my bag and slid off my chair as I started to the door only to be stopped by Charlie grabbing my arm lightly. I turned back to them with a snarl before covering my mouth and trying to pull away.

"Nym, it's ok they're just going to take you home."

I yanked my arm harder and eventually Charlie relented as I stumbled quickly away. It took a second to regain my footing before the two people by the door and hesitantly tried to go around them. Before I could get a chance though one of them knelt down and blocked me.

"Hey there, are you lost out here sweetie?"

"Just let me go."

He sighed lightly and took off his hat brushing a hand through his greasy hair.

"We aren't trying to get you in trouble or anything, we just want to help you."

"I don't need help."

He nodded slightly and looked up to his friend who sighed before also kneeling down.

"Kids can't just be going around town like this in the middle of the evening. It isn't safe for you. Please just come along and we will make sure you get wherever you're going safely."

Trying to ignore them, I took a glance past to where the door was. I could make it if I just squeezed by them. So as they continued to try to talk me down I prepared to leap through their defenses. Then I did it. For a moment I thought I got away from them before I felt a light tug on my shirt collar.

"Let me go!"

I swung my arms and kicked roughly trying to get away. As I flailed around, my hat slipped a bit from my head and I went to catch it but to no avail. I started screaming and crying as they apologized to the crowd in the restaurant. For a moment my eyes went over Char- lie and Niko seeing they were upset and a bit panicked. But there was something else as I slowly stopped flailing and raised my hands up to cover my ears; their hearts were pounding... was it fear?

"Just please calm down, we aren't here to h- w- what are you?"

Tears filled my eyes as anxiety took me from every- thing around me and I slumped to the floor not fighting anymore. My arms were now covering my head entirely as I shook from sobs.

"I- I'm sorry... I'm sorry... I'll go..."

Experiment 17 | Questions

I sat there quietly in the back of the car the men had escorted me to. Charlie and Niko had come outside to see me off but I didn't have the heart to look at them. As we pulled away, I held my hat to my head and squeezed it lightly. It hadn't even been a day and I had already been caught by people I didn't even know. My eyes wandered around the car before glancing out the window. For a moment I looked out at the world passing us by before my crimson eyes came to glare at me through the reflection of the glass as if taunting me.

"Sooooo…"

One of the men awkwardly shuffled around in his chair to get a look at me.

"What's your name?"

I sat quietly trying to pretend I couldn't hear him.

"Alright… um… my name is Dennis. Good to meet you."

"Dennis, just let her be for now. I am sure she's in shock."

I heard some mumbles back and forth before the car fell silent once more. That's how it remained until we arrived at a large boxy building with a big sign that read Central Lemmings Police Station. As the car pulled in, Dennis awkwardly shifted to look at me again before getting out and shutting his door. His friend followed and did the same.

I couldn't tell exactly what was being said but I could see that the two of them were arguing outside of the car about something. Thoughts about being locked away like I had been as a child and having experiments done on me popped into my mind and I shivered. Just as the thought consumed me a light thump came against the glass of the window before my door opened. Hesitantly, I stepped out of it clenching my bag in one hand and holding my hat down with the other.

"If you will just follow us inside, we need to ask a few questions."

Taking a deep breath, I did as I was told and followed the two of them inside. It was a rather plain place with several other people dressed similarly to the two who had picked me up. I was led along to a small table in a room and given a cup of water and a small plate of cookies. Dennis then slid into the chair across from me as his friend stood next to me.

"So, Nym. It is Nym right?"

A bit baffled by how he knew my name, I nodded lightly.

"How old are you Nym?"

I shrugged lightly. It wasn't something I was sure of.

"Right. Well, Nym, we heard that you were looking a bit lost and didn't seem to know where your parents were. Would you say that's about right?"

My heart was pounding in my chest and I shrugged hesitantly. He sighed in response and took a cookie, biting into it then gesturing for me to take one with a smile. It was hard to tell if it was genuine or not but I did take a cookie. But upon bringing it to my mouth, I found it contained chocolate and quickly set it aside to their apparent confusion.

"Allergic," I mumbled softly.

"Oh erm... sorry about that."

"I- it's ok... so am I in trouble...? Am I gonna be locked up?"

His smile faded in favor of a soft worried look.

"No, no we aren't going to do that."

He stole a look at his friend who held up his hands and stepped away.

"That being said. Where are you from? You from around here?"

I nodded nervously.

"Good. And your parents? Where are they?"

"Mom's dead… Father is in the hospital."

He nodded and jotted something down into a notebook he had on the table.

"Sorry to hear that Nym. Is that how you got lost? You left the hospital?"

I shook my head nervously.

"Well, was anyone watching you?"

There was a long pause in the conversation before he asked again.

"Y- yeah… there was…"

He nodded.

"Alright, and what is their name?"

"M- Mary…"

Again he jotted something down.

"I'm sure Mary is worried. Do you think so?"

A pit formed in my stomach and I felt sick as tears built in my eyes.

"It's alright Nym. Can you tell us her full name?"

My head shook as I pulled my legs up to my chest.

"And your father's name?"

"Witherspoon..."

He frowned lightly and sighed, writing something else and tearing it out to pass to his friend who left the room. He then grinned softly at me and sat back in his chair as if relaxing slightly.

"I see. So then Nym, how did you end up separated from Mary?"

My hand raised to my head and began scratching lightly at it as my eyes wandered away from Dennis.

"I... I ran away..."

"I see... and did something happen?"

"Father is in the hospital."

His gaze wandered as if in thought before he continued.

"Right... So why did you run?"

I anxiously leaned on the table and drew with my finger on it.

"I didn't know what to do... it all happened so fast... I don't know what's gonna happen to me."

"You are worried who's going to take care of you?"

I nodded and laid my head flat on the table causing my hat to droop, half falling off my ears. Sluggishly, I moved to readjust it caring a bit less now that they had already seen it.

"Is it because of your... condition?"

I nodded again some as I tried to sit up.

"May I see, Nym?"

Slowly, I grabbed the hat and dragged it off of my head. He looked at me as I shivered lightly. After a few moments he took a breath and jotted something down before continuing.

"How did this happen?"

"Father. I was born this way."

He nodded with a frown as a light knock came at the door. A petite girl peaked her head in and went to speak before noticing my ears. She then came in fully and walked over to get a closer look.

"Wow, they look very real, impressive."

She smiled warmly while looking between me and Dennis before realizing that she had said something silly and setting a paper down. Then looking back to me.

"So you like animals?"

I shrunk into myself and clenched at the top of my head. As my hands ran over my ears I could hear the beating of the girl's heart increase. Her steps came after as she slowly backed away from me.

"A- anyways. We found the hospital her dad is at, sir."

He nodded.

"Thank you, Marcos."

The girl nodded back and stole another glance at me before doing a little bow and leaving. Dennis gave me a warm smile and got up to step out of the room leaving me alone in silence.

Experiment 18 | Return

I sat there alone with my thoughts for a little while, wondering what was going to happen to me. The thought was still blooming into anxiety when the door to the room swung open. I nervously looked towards the opening to find Mary standing there looking out of breath and rather upset. As she approached, I shrunk into my self fearfully shaking as she pulled me into a hug.

"I'm so glad you're ok Nym."

My shaking continued and I was quiet, but I returned the hug before starting to cry.

"Y- you aren't mad...?"

She pulled away and held her hands to my face, meeting my eyes as she did so.

"No. I'm sorry if you thought I would be."

I wiped away at my eyes to get rid of the tears and hid away my eyes best I could.

"So what now...? I don't really have a home to go back to..."

"Oh Nym, your father isn't gone. He's just a bit under the weather."

"But he's going to die, isn't he?"

She didn't look at me for a moment, but then nodded faintly.

"I won't lie to you Nym... he isn't doing so well right now, but that doesn't mean there isn't a small chance."

"And what about those people who wanted to talk to me? Are they gonna take me away?"

Her face twisted into a frown and she let out a soft sigh.

"I'm sorry Nym."

"Can't I just stay with you?"

She hung her head low and shook it.

"I'm not family, Nym."

"But you could adopt me couldn't you?"

"I could try."

For a brief moment my heart felt lighter and I smiled meekly.

"*Try*. I can't promise anything Nym."

Hesitantly I nodded, still daring to smile even at the thought.

"But for now let's get you home ok?"

I nodded again and got up to follow her out with my bag over my shoulder. Most of the people in the building stopped to look at me as we went, my hat now off of my head. Add to that the ruffling at the back of my skirt and I'm sure it was quite the sight to everyone there. But soon we made it to the car and shuffled into it. It was a long and quiet ride back to the house and neither of us said much of anything. As we pulled up I saw that there were other cars in the driveway and suddenly felt nervous again. Mary seemed to notice this and laid a hand on my shoulder.

"It's ok, they just needed to finish their talk with you. You'll be fine."

I anxiously followed her up the steps and into the building as we went towards the dining room. When we entered, we found two people sitting and talking between themselves only for them to stop as we came in.

"Is she alright?"

It was directed to Mary as though I couldn't answer myself.

"She is. Just a bit shaken up is all."

Timidly, I took a seat at the table and tried to hide myself behind my hat I had in my hand.

"So… would you like to talk to us about why you ran away?"

"I um… I don't know…"

The two people sitting across from me stole a glance at one another.

"It's ok, we aren't angry with you."

I nodded slowly and took a breath.

"I was scared…"

"What were you scared of?"

"Being alone…"

Again they glanced at each other then to Mary before looking back at me.

"You know, Nym. There is a place for kids who…"

He took a long pause like he wasn't sure what to say.

"Need somewhere else to go."

"Do you really think someone would choose to have a kid like me, sir…?"

His hands interlocked and he squeezed them lightly as he stood up, stepping away from the table. The lady with him then moved to be across from me as she made a face towards her friend.

"I don't know about my partner Nym, but you seem like a good kid, and I think a parent would be lucky to have someone like you."

My cheeks felt slightly red at the sincerity in the person's voice. I curled up in my chair in response.

"That being said... is there anything else about your time living here you wanted to tell us about Nym?"

A bit worriedly I shrugged then nodded slowly.

"Well um..."

My eyes wandered down to my hands.

"I- I didn't want to give up my... my claws."

She nodded and wrote something down.

"And I want to be able to go around the house when I want to and go play with friends outside of school and ..."

By this point I was fully sobbing but tried to continue anyways.

"A- and- I want to just have a normal life l- like Chloe and the other kids..."

I grabbed hold of the sides of my messy hair and tucked away into my lap. A light hand rubbed on my back gently. There was some shuffling and writing in the room causing me to look up again. The man had retaken his seat and the lady was writing much more than usual. Before long, both of them got up again and packed away their things.

"Well, it's getting a bit late and you should get to bed. We should get going."

"But I don't even have school tomorrow..."

Mary gave me a light look of scolding and I nodded in return.

"All the same it may be a busy day."

Mary nodded to the two people as they got ready to head out before walking them to the door. When they exited the room it set in how much I had said. As I heard the door close I turned to see Mary coming back into the dining room.

"Whatever happens Nym, I think it will be good for you."

I nodded halfheartedly but I wasn't sure if I believed that.

Experiment 19 | Closure?

Morning came as it often did; abruptly. There was a soft knock on my door as I sat up in bed to see Mary peek in. Her faint smile told me it was likely going to be another long day. Shortly thereafter I was up and getting ready. After I got dressed, Mary handed me the hat and gestured for me to follow her out the door. When we got outside to the car I finally broke the silence between us.

"Where are we going?"

"To the hospital."

For a moment I stopped only halfway into the car before continuing to sit. It hadn't occurred to me that I would be seeing my father again considering the events of the prior day. Even worse, I wasn't sure I wanted to see him.

"Are you going to be ok with this?"

I nodded meekly, trying to ignore the dread building within as the car pulled out of the drive. As we went down the road we passed a lot of areas I hadn't noticed reminding me of my escapades the day before. It had become clear to me how small my world had been up to now. Maybe all of this would be a good thing after all? Just as the thought hit me, I was brought out of it by a tap on the window.

"We're here Nym."

I got out of the car and moseyed towards the entrance of the building. It was dim inside with some lights flickering faintly. There was an overwhelming smell that hit me as we entered and I had to hold my nose. In some ways, it reminded me of the room I knew when I was younger with the same sterile nature to it. While we walked down the hall to where my father was, the white walls and eerie fluorescent lights made my heart pound faster and faster. I was starting to regret having come at all.

Finally, we came to a door and entered where my father's bed was. The room was much like the rest of the building. Dim, white, and sterile but a warm light brightened it ever so slightly through a small window on the far side. The man in the bed didn't seem like my father. He seemed old, decrepit and meek. For a brief moment, I thought we had found the wrong room until the man raised a brow at me and sat up waving me over.

"Didn't expect to see you here."

His voice was rough and an equally rough cough followed it. I backed up slightly and glanced at the door behind me. It wasn't right, none of this felt right.

"Come closer kid, I won't do anything to you."

Following a nudge from Mary, I hesitantly approached keeping a healthy distance from the bed he was sat in.

"I'm sorry Nym."

His hoarse voice almost sounded sincere but I didn't dare believe it.

"It doesn't matter."

"It matters to me."

"I don't care!"

My hand flew up to my mouth and covered it in an instant at the realization I had raised my voice. Father just sighed and sat up though his face was painted with shock as if he wasn't expecting me to talk back after so long. I slowly backed away from the bed until I bumped into the wall and slid down it.

"So... that's how it is then? I suppose I should have expected as much from you."

Solemnly, I pulled my legs up to my chest and looked away from where he sat.

"What did you expect? After everything... what I am ... did you t-"

Small tears trickled down my cheeks.

"Did you think... I would be sad?"

He shook his head then smiled faintly. His smile pained me deeply as if it mocked me for feeling anything for the poor, weak man in front of me. Why did I have to feel for such a horrible person?

"I don't know what I expected Nym. I'm not sure I expected to be here, in this place, with you still so young ... so pathetic..."

"I- I'm just a kid you- you- you crappy human being..."

At some point my words shifted from pitiful and pouting to something more bitter and angry. My eyes were fiercely peering at him now as I wiped away tears and continued.

"You almost make me glad I wasn't born like you or how you wanted me to be."

His eyes were intense as they looked at me, almost as though they looked through me. He sighed heavily and turned away from me without saying another word. At that point, I found my way back up to my feet and went to leave, stopping for a moment in the doorway.

"Goodbye father..."

Taking a deep breath I left the room back to the hall where I broke down and stumbled to the floor, hitting it in frustration. Mary came to my side and hugged me loosely as I leaned into her. We sat there for a short while before finally getting up to leave back to the car. It had only been a few minutes of my life that we had been there, but I needed it, I needed to walk away from him on my own. As we got into the car I laid back in the chair rubbing at my still watery eyes.

"Hey Nym?"

"Yeah?"

"You did really well in there."

My head slumped and I looked out the window.

"No... I just stooped to his level... he's just an old man who's gonna die soon. I didn't want to give him anything after all of this."

"Nym, you're just a kid, you said so yourself. No one expects you to get everything right all the time and on days like today... well... a lot of kids wouldn't be able to do what you just did in there."

I let a small smile form on my face and brushed my hand over my nose.

"Thank you... for everything."

The remainder of the drive was quiet again but before too long we had made it back to the house. When the car stopped, we both sat there as if expecting one or the other to say something, but in the end we both went up to the door without saying a word. Once inside I set down my bag and gave a long look around the house. I went from one room to the next knowing soon I would likely never see any of it again.

The thought was somewhat calming to me. So much of my time there had been painful and every step around reminded me of that pain. Before I knew it, I found myself in my father's study, slowly walking around and looking at things I didn't notice before. It wasn't long before I came to Subject 16. It had haunted me the first time I saw it; the thought I could've ended up like them. Now I looked at them and wondered if they were luckier.

"I know it may not feel like it right now Nym, but someday things are going to be ok."

I turned to look at Mary and tried to smile. Deep down I think I knew she was right... I hoped she was right. But looking back at Subject 16, I still had that wandering thought. After a long while I took a breath and placed a hand on the case before walking away back up towards my room.

Experiment 20 | What's Next?

After sitting on my bed for nearly two hours I finally dug out my notebook to start drawing in hopes of getting my mind off of everything that was happening. As I drew, I felt a bit at peace with it all... at least I thought I did until looking back at my sketches. Messy jagged lines were scattered across the page in incoherent forms; I had almost pressed clean through the paper in spots.

In a fit of annoyance, I added to the drawing violently before throwing the papers to the floor and slumping down into my hands. Then came a sudden knock on the door. I tried to shake off my frustrations and wipe away my tears before the door inevitably creaked open. My eyes wandered over to find Mary standing there with Janie and Baxter. Suddenly, I felt very self-conscious of how I looked and what I was doing.

"Hello Nym, mind if we come in a minute?"

I wiped my eyes again then nodded, averting my eyes from them.

"I see you did some drawing?"

My face felt warm as I got off the bed to pick up the pictures. Janie knelt down and picked one up herself as I reached for it. Not knowing what to do, I leaned back to sit against the bed on the floor, somewhat hiding behind the drawings already in my hands. She turned the picture she grabbed around to show it to me after a few moments.

"Can you tell me what this is supposed to be?"

I shook my head nervously. She smiled and went to hand back the picture which I took hastily.

"It's ok, you don't have to talk about it if you don't want to. Are you doing ok? We heard you visited your dad earlier today."

Again I shook my head.

"I- it's been on my mind a lot I guess. I said some things I wanted to say and did things I wanted to do... but..."

"Doesn't feel great?"

For a third time I shook my head.

"I thought I'd feel more... I don't know... calm? But it feels like my insides are all mixed up and nothing feels right."

She nodded in return.

"Well, you know, lots of kids who have been through what you have felt that way."

"There are other kids like me...?"

Perhaps realizing what I meant, she frowned lightly.

"In a way, yes. Not exactly like you, but they have been through some similar things."

"How so...?"

She brushed her hand through her hair as if thinking on something.

"Well sweetie, what I mean is not everyone is lucky enough to have kind and loving parents and sometimes when they are really mean we come by and try to help those kids out. Kids like you Nym."

My hands gripped the pictures tighter and I took a breath as I got to my feet.

"So um... how do you help then?"

She snuck a glance to Mary who nodded.

"Well Nym, when an adult isn't doing the best with their kids anymore we come by and help them find a new, hopefully happier home."

"Right... so you're taking me away..."

Mary looked over to me and smiled weakly and I gazed back. It wasn't as though I didn't know this was happening, but somehow talking about it like this makes it so much more... real?

"When?"

"Well... usually it would be a few months, but considering your dads health concerns... it very likely could be sooner."

Feeling a bit sick, I nodded.

"Will I be staying around here?"

"In the same town maybe, but I can't guarantee anything."

Maybe? I might not even be allowed to stay near my friend...

"Ok... is that what you two wanted to talk to me about?"

She smiled warmly and nodded.

"We wanted to sit down with you and Miss Mary here to discuss some stuff regarding what's next and what may or may not happen."

"So there's more?"

"Not much, no."

She stood up and went towards the door waving her partner to follow along. As they stepped out Mary turned to help me up and lead me out with them. We went downstairs to the living room and took a seat around the couch. My nerves had picked up again as I looked around the room before focusing on Janie as she went to speak.

"So, we haven't had much of a chance to speak with your dad about it, but Nym, do you know of any family or extended family of yours?"

Meekly I shook my head.

"I don't think I have anyone else... at least not blood wise."

For a moment when I said it I couldn't help but find myself looking at Mary and somewhere in my mind thinking about Chloe too.

"Ok Nym. Do you have any allergies?"

"Chocolate?"

She nodded and smiled at my seeming confusion.

"Any medical issues?"

"Um... other than this?"

I gestured to my ears and tail. She wrote down some things in her notepad.

"Any other health related things you know of?"

Mary cleared her throat.

"With all due respect ma'am, isn't this sort of stuff on file already?"

Janie frowned.

"We haven't found any official documentation on Nym unfortunately. We didn't even know she existed until we were called to this location. If not for some paperwork her father had, we would have assumed the worst for her being here."

Suddenly my heart sank.

"I... wait... but wasn't I born in a hospital?"

My breath picked up in a bit of a panic as I turned to look at Mary again.

"Calm down Nym, it's going to be ok."

"B- but I thought I was born in a hospital? A- and... I mean... I didn't even know... is my name even Nym?"

Deep in my stomach, I felt sick and held a hand over my mouth.

"Nym... it's ok. You're Nym. That is you. Even if some paper somewhere doesn't perfectly line up with that."

Janie sighed lightly.

"I'm sorry Nym, I didn't mean to upset you. We just needed to make sure we had the right information for you. We were going to have you taken to the doctors but considering your background we weren't sure how you'd do there."

I nodded slightly in response.

"I- I'm not a lab rat... I didn't think I was..."

Both Mary and Janie shared a worried and maybe sad look.

"I- I really was just an experiment wasn't I...?"

The room was quiet and everyone didn't look at me.

"My father... he really didn't love me at all did he..."

No one answered, they didn't have to.

"I... I think I just want to go back to my room..."

"Nym..."

"It's ok, I'll be fine"

I said it with a soft smile that was quivering weakly as tears swelled in my eyes. Quickly, I brushed at them but to no avail so instead I just let them fall as I got up.

"Nym?"

"I... really wanted to believe... that you were right and somewhere he cared..."

My words trailed off as I slowly stumbled my way back to my room. Around me the others still talked and maybe reached out to me, but I couldn't hear it clearly anymore.

Experiment 21 | Last Day of First School

I didn't want to do anything or talk to anyone when the following morning came around. Mary checked on me a few times as the day dragged on but never made me leave my room. Good. I didn't want to leave, I just wanted to be left alone. So it was that the rest of the day slowly came and went until nighttime again. My head was aching with the mixed thoughts swimming in it and over time the thoughts gave way to sleep.

I rolled off the bed as I slipped out of dreams and nightmares, thudding down to the floor. Looking at the clock, I realized it was still very early in the morning with school still being hours off. Trying not to think too much about it I got off the floor and began getting ready for my day. A light knock came at the door by the time I was packing up my bag, bringing in Mary smiling meekly to me.

"I see you already got up and ready for school... you know you don't have to go, right?"

"But I want to... I think I need to get away from here."

From the look on Mary's face, I could tell she was concerned in my comment.

"Don't worry, I won't run away again."

Her face softened back to a weary smile but she nodded and came over to give me a hug.

"Sorry... I didn't mean to worry you." My breath was heavy as I responded.

"It's ok, I know this is all very overwhelming to you."

I nodded lightly and went to grab my bag.

"Can we just go now?"

She snuck a peek at the clock then nodded while leading the way out the door. I followed down the stairs as I did most mornings and out to the car. On our way to the school, she briefly stopped to grab some breakfast for us and let me eat as she drove. We finally arrived at the front of the school before too much longer. For a while, I sat quietly in the car until Mary almost left before shaking off my anxiety and getting out to go inside. I stole one more look at Mary who smiled warmly at me as I disappeared through the doors.

The hall seemed so much more daunting than it had lately as I walked along with my head hung low. From time to time, I would bump into people who would get angry with me as I tried to ignore them while making my way to the classroom. I found my way to my desk and sat, feeling distant from what was going on around me. Suddenly a familiar hand found its way to my shoulder and I looked over to see Chloe starting to cry as I did.

"Oh gosh Nym... what happened?"

It felt almost as though I was choking on nothing as I tried to answer and instead dug out my notebook to write for her. I shakily wrote out what had happened and what might still happen before slowly sliding it over to her, letting my head lay down on my desk. With my head down, I heard the shuffling of the paper and an audible gasp come from Chloe.

"Nym... I'm so sorry..."

I sluggishly lifted my head off the desk and looked at Chloe with a pitiful attempt of a smile while shaking my head. Just then, the teacher sat everyone down to start class. It was a dreadfully long lesson that day. Even knowing how to do most of what she had us doing, I couldn't seem to focus on anything that was given. After what felt like a full school days' worth of hours, lunch eventually came around.

Chloe walked with me closely, rubbing at my back and trying to calm me down from the earlier events of the day. Though it didn't really feel like it was helping, I greatly appreciated the attempt. As soon as we arrived at the cafeteria and found some seats, Chloe went to talk again.

"So um... wanna talk about it?"

Quietly I shook my head before taking a breath.

"I..."

I tried hard to fend off the tears that were threatening to come out again as I continued.

"Just not sure what to say."

"It's gotta be really hard for you..."

I nodded meekly.

"I'm just scared I won't be here anymore... that I will have to find a new friend somewhere else..."

Chloe frowned deeply and started getting teary eyed.

"We'll still be friends Nym, won't we?"

Fully crying now but with a wide smile, I nodded fiercely.

"Of course we'll still be friends."

She returned a smile wiping tears from her eyes.

"I'm gonna miss you Nym... but maybe you won't have to go?"

My shoulders slumped slightly.

"Yeah... I guess it could happen..."

The bell rang, ending the moment for us and ushering everyone back to their classrooms. We saw scribbling on my desk as we entered and approached. It wasn't uncommon, but this one was clearly related to what had been going on today. *"Go away dog girl"* it read in sharp crimson letters. For a few moments I stood there peering at it before looking intensely and angrily around the room. Several people were staring and snickering to themselves.

Back in a corner one small group of boys were chattering especially loud. There was red ink smeared on one of their shirts. Without much thought I went over and pushed his desk over with him still in it. He tumbled down like a bunch of bricks onto the ground, rubbing at his side as he tried to get up. Again, I looked to the class around me this time hearing their snickering turning to silence and light mumbles.

Then a fist came at the back of my head and landed, causing me to stumble forward and grasping at where the hit landed. I turned to glare at the boy who had cheaply hit me and he cowered back. Just as I was about to hit him in retaliation, the teacher came over to break it up.

"What is going on over here?"

"This girl is crazy; she just came over and shoved Lucas' desk down."

"Only cus he wrote on my desk..."

I mumbled it quietly under my breath knowing I was likely not winning this fight. But to my surprise the teacher walked over to my desk and ran a finger over it, smearing the ink lightly.

"Is this true?"

Lucas, who was still picking himself up, leaned on one of the desks and averted his eyes before silently nodding his confirmation. My ears twitched in surprise at the situation and I stole a look to the teacher who had a hand over her face.

"Ok, both of you, detention after school today."

My ears drooped low as she said, as if this day couldn't get any worse.

"Yes ma'am... sorry..."

Lucas almost looked more disheartened than I felt. Maybe it was his first time in detention? So it was that as classes wrapped up that day I found myself sitting across the room from Lucas in detention with a teacher I didn't know watching us. They had called his parents and mine... called Mary... and now here we were. Lucas kept stealing looks at me until finally throwing a piece of paper over to the floor near me.

It looked like the teacher wasn't paying much attention so I bent down picking up the crumpled bit and opened it with expectations of more insults. But to my surprise I found nothing of the sort. *"You were kind of cool today"* it read in the same sharp handwriting on my desk. With confusion across my face I raised an eye towards the clearly dumb boy who sat away from me. He smiled meekly back to me as if he didn't just treat me like crap earlier in the day.

Hastily I wrote a small note of my own to throw back to him that read *"leave me alone you dummy"* and threw it back missing by a good amount. Taking multiple glances at the teacher he leaned down to pick it up, almost face planting as he did so and causing me to laugh faintly. His face was priceless upon reading the note.

Before long though the paper hit the ground near my feet again and I let out a sigh as I picked it up to read it. *"Sorry about earlier."* I was so confused reading it. Maybe he was just trying to clear his conscience. Instead of replying, I left the paper where it was and laid my head down on my desk. But just then another paper landed by my feet causing me to let out yet another sigh and bend down to pick it up. *"Are you really gonna be going away soon?"*

"Why did he care?" I thought as I looked over to him. His stupid smile on his stupid face was still there. With a bit of frustration I took the note and jotted down on the back of it *"Does it matter?"* and then threw it towards him. For a moment it looked like he wasn't going to pick it up but before long he did. His smile turned to a frown and he wrote another thing before throwing it back.

"I think so." As I read it, the timer at the front of the class rang telling us it was time to leave. I quickly grabbed my bag all too happy to get away from Lucas. Once I was in the hallway though he hurried behind me to catch up.

"Hey, so, really though are you going?"

"Leave me alone."

"I said I was sorry."

"Just stop."

"I'm trying to be nice"

"Stop! I said stop!"

He did so as I continued to walk away from him clutching my bag. For a moment before I headed out the front door I turned to see him meekly waving after me and briefly smiling. What a stupid face.

As I exited the building, I found Mary outside waiting for me in the car and went over to her. I could feel her questioning gaze on me as if to ask *"why did you do that?"*. I laid my head against the window looking away from her in an attempt to put off the conversation. It didn't last long though as she cleared her throat to get my attention.

"I'm sorry... I shouldn't have gotten into a fight..."

"It isn't that Nym."

Upon looking at her again I saw something different; she seemed concerned and worried.

"What is it then...?"

She took a deep breath and brushed her hair back with one of her hands.

"It's your father Nym."

I suddenly felt sick.

"I- is he... dead?"

For a moment she stole a glance at me before nodding a confirmation.

"So that's it... I'm going away now..."

Experiment 22 | To Whatever's Next

Our drive continued in a solemn silence as we headed back to what was my home. I moseyed up to the door when we arrived, a bit nervous to go inside and see it all even once more. But inevitably I entered and slowly walked about the place here and there. It wasn't until I came to my room though that it truly set in that this was likely it. I looked at the drawings I had made either etched in the walls or pinned to the ceiling before sitting on the bed once more. While I sat trying in vain not to sob at it all a light knock came at the door. It was Mary as it had been many times before. It may be Mary for the last time.

"Nym... I said it before, but somehow this will all be ok."

My hands rubbed at my eyes as I shook my head. How could I believe anything would be ok after all of this? Soon she shuffled over and sat next to me wrapping an arm around me in a gentle hug as she let me sob into her.

"W- what now...?"

I looked up to her still crying with a look of exasperated expectation on my face.

"Well... we need to start getting you packed for one. They'll be coming by this evening to get you."

"S- so soon?"

"I'm sorry Nym... I'm not your legal guardian so I can't keep you any longer than that."

"Couldn't you just become my legal guardian...?"

Her head slumped and she looked away from me.

"It isn't that simple Nym."

"But why not?"

She brushed a hand through my hair softly, stopping briefly at one of my ears then moving over it.

"I wish I could tell you Nym, sometimes that's just how life is."

Not liking that answer much, I pulled away from her and started getting my things together. I realized how little I really had after stacking up my drawings and grabbing the clothes out of my closet. It only filled one bag. I let out a soft sigh as I finished zipping up my bag before getting up and taking another look at my sketching on the walls. Hesitantly I ran a hand over some of the ones I did before finally stepping away.

"Is this the last time I'll be here?"

Mary frowned lightly and nodded.

"Ok... I think I am ok with that."

Her frown shifted into a soft smile.

"You will be, you're a tough kid after all."

After trying to return the smile I picked up my bag and brought it down the stairs with me. I set it down at the bottom of the stairs then went to the study for one more look at my would-be sibling. While I stood there in front of them in that little glass box, I heard footsteps come into the room. Looking over, I found Janie in the doorway.

"Hey Nym..."

She walked over and stood next to me looking over at the case.

"That's-"

I nodded meekly.

"The one before me. They didn't make it."

She seemed a bit bothered by it as I answered.

"Do you look at them often?"

"Not until all this. I tried not to think about them much."

"What changed?"

"I think I did?"

She nodded slightly and rested a hand on my shoulder. It felt almost wrong that this person I barely knew was doing this, but I let her anyway. I wasn't in the mood to argue about anything.

"Are you all packed?"

I nodded slowly.

"Are you ready to go?"

"I don't know if I'll ever be ready for this."

She sighed lightly.

"I understand that, sometimes in life we aren't ready for things and all we can do is keep moving forward through it all."

Meekly I nodded and turned to look at her.

"I like that. I want to keep moving."

Again, I stole a glance at the glass case.

"I don't want to end up like them."

"You won't, I'm sure of it."

"Can you say that? With what I am? Will anyone want me?"

She smiled softly.

"I said before you're a good kid. I think anyone would be lucky to have you."

"But that isn't the same as thinking anyone will want me."

Her smile twisted into a frown and she let out a sigh.

"I wish I could tell you that, but I don't really know."

"Right…"

"Are you ready to go?"

"I um… can I go say goodbye to Mary first?"

Janie nodded and went to the front of the house to wait for me as I went around to find Mary. When I found her she was sitting at the dining room table looking melancholic. Upon seeing me she wiped tears away from her eyes and smiled at me weakly.

"Hey, how are you doing?"

"I- I… better I guess?"

She nodded lightly.

"That's good, but you don't need to be better now if you aren't, ok? Feelings aren't a bad thing."

Again the tears came and I nodded once more.

"Will I see you again?"

She smiled warmly.

"You probably will, I hope."

With that I gave her a hug and then left the room to go meet Janie in the front of the house.

"Ready to go?"

L. J. Bomba

Taking one last look around the house I nodded for a final time.

"As much as I can be."

Epilogue

The beeping of the alarm clock next to me had me rolling out of bed as it had many prior mornings in the past two months. I had grown more accustomed to the loud and busy weekend mornings around the orphanage I was staying in. By noon, many of the chores would be done then it was on to do any school work we had from the week prior. Luckily, I had already finished mine during lunch at school so I was left alone in one of the rooms sitting and writing in a corner.

Several of the pictures I drew were of things that had happened since I had arrived. Other kids I had known before they had been adopted or some of the older kids who would likely be with me until they left. All and all it wasn't so bad, the owners of the building were kind as well as several people who worked there. As I continued to sketch, I flipped back to an earlier page with a picture of Chloe in many shades of red. It made me sad to look back on, but at least I knew whatever she was doing we were still friends.

"Hey Nym, yah drawing again?"

From my paper I glanced up at the young girl who was sitting across from me also on the floor. It was Yarna, one of the other kids who had been around since I came in. Her scruffy red hair hung low into her face half masking her eyes. I pulled some of it back and turned around a recent picture of her I had drawn.

"Oh wow! It's me!"

She took the sheet and investigated it carefully as if it were some fine piece of art and she was a critic. I couldn't help but giggle to myself as she closed an eye and held it at a distance to get some sort of alternate look at it.

"I don't know how you get so much out of one color, it is really cool though."

"Thanks."

Though I had been there for a bit I still wasn't very talkative with most of the other kids. I mostly just tried to keep my head down and hat on. It wasn't as though many of the others weren't aware of me, but it helped me feel like they weren't.

"Oh! How are they looking today?"

Quietly, I laughed to myself looking around before slowly working the gloves off of my hands. Small claws had been growing in where my old ones had been cut and were getting pretty long at that point.

"They're so long now!"

It had only been a few weeks since she last pestered me about them, but I felt the need to humor her since she was a very sweet girl.

"What does it feel like?"

"What?"

"Being like you? I mean like... an erm..."

"Animal girl?"

Her head hung low and she looked away from me in shame. I knew she didn't mean anything by it and I ignored the twinge of pain that came with the question to smile at her.

"It feels... like I can hear all sorts of sounds? Like I can smell so much in the air around us? Like I might hurt someone if I'm not careful... It feels like me."

She looked at me with somewhat wide eyes and nodded her understanding.

"Sounds like a lot."

"It has been... for a lot of my life."

"And you're ok?"

"I will be."

My smile became a bit fuller then. As it often did when I thought about Mary.

"Well um… I'm gonna go downstairs with some of the others I think."

I nodded and let her run along as I leaned back against the wall reminiscing on better parts of my life that past year or so. Time seemed to stand still some days and others it felt like it had been no time at all. While I was lost in thought a soft knock came on the wall snapping me out of it.

"Nym?"

It was Miss Lilia who worked at the orphanage.

"H- hi… may I help you?"

She shook her head then smiled warmly.

"There is someone here who wants to talk with you."

Almost as though the words didn't register, I rubbed at my eyes then ears.

"Sorry, say again?"

"Someone wants to see you."

"Like *see* me?"

Now she nodded her warm smile widening as she watched realization grow on my face.

"B- but why would they want to… didn't y'all tell them about me?"

"We did… it's actually the thing that made them want to see you even more."

My ears lowered as anxiety picked up. That couldn't be good. They could be someone who wanted to see a creature like me. Or they could be someone who wants to experiment... I shivered lightly at the thought until Lilia nudged me.

"Hey it'll be ok."

"How can you know that?"

"Well... it seems this person knows you or seems to."

Knows me? Suddenly my heart picked up in pace as I got up to hurry down the stairs to see this person who knew me. As I came out into the hall and down it I came out to the room where new parents usually talked to the people who worked there. There sitting in one of the chairs was indeed someone I knew, but it wasn't who I expected.

"Nym?"

"N- Niko?"